'Marry me,' Kyle said.

For a second the words filled Liane with an indescribable pleasure. Still dizzy with the passion of his kisses, her only thought was to say yes. And then her eyes cleared and she saw him looking down at her.

'Marry me,' he said again.

In a rush, memory came flooding back. And then she had her hands against his chest and was pushing herself away from him.

'Never!'

Dear Reader

This month, I would like to ask you to think about the kind of heroine you would like to find in our stories. Do you think she should be sweet and gentle, on the look-out for a man who will be able to care for and nurture her, or should the heroine be able to give as good as she gets, throwing punch for punch, and quite capable of standing up for herself? If you have any opinions on this matter please let us know, so that we can continue to give you the books you want to read!

The Editor

Rosemary Carter was born in South Africa, but has lived in Canada for many years with her husband and her three children. Although her home is on the prairies, not far from the beautiful Rockies, she still retains her love of the South African bushveld, which is why she likes to set her stories there. Both Rosemary and her husband enjoy concerts, theatre, opera and hiking in the mountains. Reading was always her passion, and led to her first attempts at writing stories herself.

Recent titles by the same author:

NIGHT OF THE SCORPION

CAPTIVE BRIDE

BY

ROSEMARY CARTER

MILLS & BOON LIMITED
ETON HOUSE, 18-24 PARADISE ROAD
RICHMOND, SURREY TW9 1SR

First published in Great Britain 1993
by Mills & Boon Limited

© Rosemary Carter 1993

Australian copyright 1993
Philippine copyright 1993
This edition 1993

ISBN 0 263 78179 8

Set in Times Roman 10 on 11¼ pt.
01-9308-52823 C

Made and printed in Great Britain

CHAPTER ONE

LIANE DUBOIS slowed the car as the long white fence came into sight. It had been a busy day in the public relations department of the winery where she worked, and usually at this time of the afternoon she was anxious to get back to her grandfather, who would be waiting for her by the window of their cottage. Today was different. With the sale of the farm finalised earlier this week, Liane knew that it was only a matter of time before the new owners arrived to take possession. She did not know their names, as the sale had been arranged through a third party, but she had promised Martin Simpson, the lawyer, to let him have all the keys tomorrow.

This was her last chance to bid a private farewell to the place which had once been her home.

The sun was setting as she drove through the tall gates with the name 'High Valley' emblazoned into the wrought-iron arch which extended from one gatepost to the other. Members of the Dubois family had lived on this land since Pierre Dubois had come to South Africa from France almost two hundred and fifty years earlier. It was almost impossible to believe that the land was now passing into other hands.

Liane took the car slowly along the road that led to the main house, a majestic drive, bordered with thick-trunked oaks, some of which Pierre Dubois had planted himself. On one side of the house was a wide brick pad; Liane had heard stories of grand parties held in another era, when the pad had been crowded with the horse-drawn buggies of the guests who had travelled out from

Cape Town. By the time her grandparents had taken over the estate, cars had replaced horses as a mode of transport, but there had never been a lack of parking space beside the house.

The brick pad was empty now. The house itself had the deserted look of a place which had not been inhabited for some time. Beneath the graceful Cape Dutch gables the windows were shuttered and closed, and the creepers climbing the walls were a little overgrown because there was nobody to trim them. Liane wondered if the new owners would love the place as the Dubois had loved it before them.

Leaving the car, she walked towards the house. She found the key with its ornamental head and inserted it into the lock of the thick wooden door. As she walked into the musty entrance hall she had a sense of endings, of history passing. After today, if she entered this house it would be only as a guest.

Slowly she walked from room to room. There was not a square inch of the house which did not hold memories: the living-room which once had been resplendent with fine furniture and paintings and rugs; the country kitchen; her grandfather's study with its panelled walls and stinkwood desk; the bedroom in which her parents had slept for too few years.

Liane came to her old room. If she closed her eyes she could picture the four-poster bed with its pink quilted bedspread, the frilled curtains and the rack which had held her collection of miniature dolls.

She walked to the window and opened it, and her eyes were caught by a nick in the wooden sill. Kyle's shoe had left that mark on the night he'd come to her room. He had slipped, she remembered, and they had worried that the thud of his landing would have woken her grandfather. The house had remained silent, and they had begun to kiss, but not for long: they had both been nervous in case her grandfather might walk in. And after a few minutes Kyle had left once more through the window.

Kyle... Six years older than Liane. Tall, dark, very thin. So handsome and so much fun. Liane had been crazily in love with him. Seventeen years old at the time, she had found herself swept on a tide of passion which had been too strong for either of them to resist. Infatuation! a maddened Gramps had shouted after the events of one terrible night. Infatuation on the part of an inexperienced young girl for a good-for-nothing lout who could never be her equal.

Overcome with grief and pain and shock, Liane had been unable to argue. Afterwards, when she had been able to think again, Kyle was gone, without so much as a forwarding address where she could reach him.

Seven years later, and never again as passionate about any man as she had been about Kyle, she wondered what would have happened if circumstances had been different. If she had been able to put up a fight.

She ran a finger along the dent in the wood, feeling its roughness against the smoothness of the sill. When the new owners moved in they would see the dent, repair it with filler and varnish the wood. The mark would disappear, and with it the last memory of Kyle. Liane was twenty-four now, it was time she let go of her own past too, let herself think of a future. It was unfair to all the men she met that a distant memory had become a standard of comparison.

She closed the window, said a silent goodbye to the room she had slept in for so many years, then quickly retraced her steps through the empty house and turned the key in the lock for the last time.

She was walking to her car when she paused in surprise. Beside her rather battered old Honda there was another car now—silver-grey, sleek and expensive-looking. As far as Liane knew, it did not belong to the lawyer or the real-estate agent.

And then she saw a man. He was coming towards her. A tall man with dark hair, broad shoulders and an easy, confident walk. He wore cream trousers and a navy shirt, and there was an expensive elegance about the casual clothes. The setting sun was behind him, its rays dazzling Liane's eyes, so that she could not see his face. A stranger—she did not have to see his features to know that; nobody in this quiet farming area looked remotely like this man. At the same time, there was something curiously familiar about him as well.

He came to a stop in front of her.

'Hello, Liane,' he said.

She looked at him in confusion. 'You know me...'

'You know me too.'

'I don't think I do. Are you sure we've met?'

'You don't remember?' His voice was mocking, his eyes hard.

She was angry all at once. He was far too self-assured, this very good-looking man. 'Should I?'

'Is seven years asking too much of your memory? Or do you only retain the important people in your life?'

In that instant she knew. In her stomach her muscles were suddenly rigid, and every nerve felt raw.

'*Kyle*?' she whispered.

'So you do remember.' Still that mocking tone.

'I've never forgotten.'

'You could have fooled me moments ago.'

She struggled for control. 'You had the advantage of me then.' With the old Kyle she had been at ease, but this hard stranger was making her feel tense and ridiculously nervous. 'This is—was—my home. You'd have known you might find me here.'

'Point taken,' he drawled.

'While you... Well, you're the last person I expected to see.'

'Ah.'

'Besides, Kyle, you've changed. You're nothing like the boy I remember.'

'Meaning I'm no longer a tousled stable-hand?'

She lifted her chin. 'Meaning you're no longer the twenty-three-year-old I once knew.'

'Knew?' One eyebrow lifted insolently. 'You make us sound like acquaintances! As I recall, we did more than nod to each other in passing.'

Liane felt her cheeks grow hot. 'I don't know why you're so hostile. All I meant was that you've changed. Your hair is shorter, your shoulders broader. I knew there was something familiar about you, but with the sun in my eyes I couldn't make out your face—and that's changed too. More than anything, though...' She stopped.

'Go on,' he prompted.

'It isn't important.'

'I'd like to hear it all the same.'

'Your whole bearing is different,' she explained. 'Your voice, your manner. I shouldn't be surprised, I suppose; seven years is a long time.'

'Circumstances made it even longer,' he said grimly.

'Circumstances?'

'Ignore that. I said we'd been more than nodding acquaintances, and you changed the subject. Have you forgotten the things we used to do together, Liane?'

Involuntarily, her hand touched her stomach, but she dropped it quickly, before he could make anything of the gesture.

'No,' she said, her voice very low, 'I haven't forgotten.'

'I wouldn't have believed you if you'd said otherwise. You were the adored granddaughter, the princess, the cosseted child who could have everything she wanted, but for all that you were never a slut. And at the time I believed I was your first man.'

Liane did not answer. She made herself stand very still as his hands went unexpectedly to her face. His thumbs pressed lightly beneath her chin and his fingers stroked a provocative path up and down her cheeks. She tried to ignore the excitement that rose inside her at his touch. For seven years she had dreamed about Kyle, had longed to be reunited with him. And now he was here.

But this was not Kyle, this insolent man with hands that knew how to ignite flames inside a woman's body. Seven years ago they had both been inexperienced, awkward and a little fumbling, passion their only guide on how to make love. Liane was a woman now, yet she was still inexperienced, for there had been few men in her life since Kyle, and none with whom she had had any desire to be intimate. The same, clearly, could not be said for him. There had been women in his life, and after all this time it made no sense at all that the knowledge hurt.

'*Was* I your first man?' he asked.

She stepped backwards, away from hands that sought to detain her.

'I was seventeen,' she said abruptly. 'I think it's obvious there'd been nobody before you.'

'And since?' he asked softly.

'That question doesn't justify an answer. My life stopped being any concern of yours a long time ago.'

Dark eyes glinted. 'Spoken like the true granddaughter of Grant Dubois. I recognise the same imperious tone.'

Could a man really have changed so much? The Kyle Avery who had once aroused such wild emotion in Liane had been a gentle person, loving, kind, funny. Not a trace in him then of the hardness and cynicism that seemed to mark him now.

'Married?' he asked.

'No.'

'Man in your life?'

His abruptness had her lifting her head. 'I thought you understood—my personal life is none of your concern.'

'I'm asking all the same.'

'All right, then—there are people I see.'

'Seriously? Engaged to any of them?'

She gave a short laugh. 'You seem to have developed the hide of an elephant, Kyle. I've made it clear I don't want to talk about my personal relationships. I haven't asked about the women in your life.'

'Interested?' he drawled.

'Not particularly,' she lied.

'I don't think you mean that.'

'We were friends once, Kyle. All right, more than friends,' she admitted as she saw the mocking amusement in his face, 'but all that was long ago. We've gone our different ways since then, and——'

'I'm not married, Liane.'

Her fingers curled into the palms of her hands, her nails cutting into the soft flesh. His eyes held hers, defying them to move away. At thirty, this new Kyle Avery was even more good-looking than the innocent young man who had looked after the horses at twenty-three. His face, merry and carefree once, was all hard lines and angles now. His jaw was firm, and his lips were surprisingly sensuous, as if he had learned a lot about women and life, and enjoyed the things he had experienced. His eyebrows were thicker than they had been, and beneath his clothes Liane had the sense of a body that was all whipcord strength and taut muscle. Only the eyes were the same, large and dark and framed with long, thick lashes. Beautiful eyes.

She shrugged. 'Some men do take their time to get married.'

'You're not curious to know why I haven't done so yet?'

'I'm only curious to know what you're doing here.'

He grinned. 'There was a time when I had a fondness for the place.'

'Did you hear it had been sold?' she asked. 'Is that why you came? To see it one last time before it passes into new hands?'

He did not answer, but the grin deepened, and the dark eyes held a wicked glint.

Suddenly Liane understood. '*You* bought High Valley?'

He let her wait a full ten seconds before he said, 'Correct.'

She stared at him, realising that it was only the shock of seeing him so unexpectedly that had kept her from guessing the truth earlier.

'Good lord . . .' she said inadequately.

'Upset?'

'Surprised,' she amended.

'I have a feeling the word is an understatement.' His tone was dry.

Anger rose inside her once more. '*Why*, Kyle? Why this particular farm?'

'I told you, I used to have a fondness for the place. In fact, I used to love it.'

'If you'd loved it, you'd have been back long ago.'

'You don't really believe that.'

The mocking tone made her uncertain. 'At least to visit...'

'I was determined not to set one foot on this land until I owned it,' he told her.

'How did you know it was for sale?' Liane demanded.

'I had an agent watching out for me.'

'A *spy*.' She bit out the words.

'Call it whatever you like.' He laughed harshly. 'Fact is, Liane, when I heard the land was for sale, I decided to buy it.'

The speed with which High Valley had been sold had been a source of surprise to both the real-estate company and Liane's grandfather. Only a few days after the farm had been placed on the market, the offer to purchase had been received—not for the full asking price, yet, on reflection, Gramps had agreed that it was preferable to accept a poor offer now rather than wait for a better offer which might never materialise—waiting being an unaffordable luxury when finances were strained.

Liane felt a pang of remorse as she remembered the hours she had spent persuading her grandfather to relinquish the farm. He had been reluctant to let High Valley go so quickly, and it seemed now that he might have been right.

'You drove a hard bargain,' she said.

'Nobody forced you to accept,' Kyle pointed out.

'I suppose your spy must have told you that Gramps wasn't in a position to hold out for too long.'

'There were things I learned.' Not a hint of apology in those hard, dark eyes.

The disastrous investment. The growing liability to cover expenses. The hailstorm which had destroyed the last harvest, and with it the last hope of saving the farm for the Dubois. Were these the things that Kyle had learned?

'We had no idea you were interested in buying High Valley,' Liane said slowly. 'To my knowledge, you were never even here to look the place over.'

'There was no need,' he explained. 'This was my home until I was twenty-three. My father lived here, and my grandfather before him. I didn't have to see High Valley to know that I wanted to own it.'

'But why did you keep your offer a secret? Why did you make the purchase through a third party?'

'I had a feeling you'd get around to that.'

'Well?' she asked tensely.

'Do you really need an explanation, Liane?'

'I'd like one, yes.'

'Right, then, suppose your grandfather had known I was the prospective buyer; do you think he'd have sold to me?'

'Kyle...' She stopped.

'An honest answer,' he insisted harshly.

'No,' she said simply, 'he wouldn't have sold to you.'

'There you have my explanation, Liane. Grant Dubois would have seen me in hell rather than let me buy his precious farm, the legacy of all those proud ancestors.'

'He's an old man, Kyle. Things have gone rather badly for us in recent years, and you may know that Gramps isn't very well.'

'Don't play on my sympathies.' There was no softening in Kyle's tone.

'He's been hurt, Kyle.'

'He never gave a damn about hurting anyone else.'

'I know he shouldn't have asked you to leave High Valley...'

'*Asked* me to leave?' The hardness in Kyle's face and tone intensified. 'There was no asking, Liane. Your grandfather threw me out—viciously. Gave me exactly an hour to get my things packed and be out of the place. Threw my father out too.'

The colour drained from Liane's cheeks as she stared at him in shock. 'I didn't know the details,' she whispered.

'Don't give me that innocent look! There's no way you couldn't have known what happened.'

'I realised there'd been some unpleasantness...'

'Unpleasantness? Nice word to describe what took place between your grandfather and myself. Still the princess, are you, Liane? You'd have known the extent of the so-called unpleasantness if you'd taken the trouble to follow the old devil to the stables that night. If you'd made even the slightest effort to intervene, maybe you could have stopped what happened.' The words were clipped, bitter, his eyes damning her as he spoke them.

Liane found it hard to meet his gaze. There were things Kyle obviously didn't know about that night—and about the days and nights and months that had followed.

'Kyle...' she began.

'Well?' The eyes that raked her face were heavy with impatience and disgust.

Liane hesitated. It shouldn't be too late to talk to him, to explain. Not too late to make him understand, at least in part, the thing that had provoked her grandfather's terrible anger. But the man looking down at her out of eyes that had the coldness of steel was not the boy she had once loved. This arrogant man bore not the slightest resemblance to the sensitive youth she had dreamed with, ridden with, loved with. She could tell him the truth, of course she could do that, but would it make any more impression on him than the news of her grandfather's ill-health? She did not think she could bear his cynicism—not where it concerned a matter that had affected her so deeply that even now, seven years later, she had never come to terms with it.

He was watching her. 'You were going to say something, Liane.'

She made herself shrug. 'It wasn't important.'

'Sure?'

She hesitated another moment, tempted to talk after all. She looked at him again, taking in the autocratic lines of the handsome face, the firmness of the lips, the inflexible set of the jaw.

Suppressing a shiver, she said, 'It was nothing that would make any difference to the way you feel.'

'If you say so.'

'I do.' Time to change the subject. 'Are you going to be farming, Kyle?'

'I have plans.'

'What kind of plans?'

'You'll hear about them as I go along,' he told her.

'I suppose I will.'

'And you, Liane, what will you do now that High Valley is no longer in family hands?'

'My life won't change,' she told him. 'I have a public relations job, and I'm good at what I do. My grandfather and I live together very quietly in a cottage just beyond the boundary of the farm. None of that will change.'

'I see.'

'I should go now.' Liane put her hand in her bag and took out her car keys. She was about to walk away when she said, 'By the way, when will you be moving in?'

'A few weeks. I expect I'll be seeing you around.'

'I expect you will,' she said lightly. The car keys clinked against the key of the house that was still in her hand. She held it out to him. 'I was going to give this to the lawyer tomorrow. I'll be giving him all the keys of the property then. But you might as well have this key now.'

His hand reached for the key, and his fingers closed around hers. As the contact brought back memories she had tried so hard to forget, Liane was overcome by a momentary dizziness. She looked at Kyle. His lips were tilted slightly at the corners, and there was a watchful look in the dark eyes. Her emotion had not been lost on him.

She took a quick breath, drew back her head, and said coolly, 'I hope you'll be very happy at High Valley.'

She did not wait for his answer. Minutes later she had started the engine of the Honda.

Liane stopped the car at the side of the cottage, but stayed behind the wheel a few seconds before opening the door to get out. Glancing into the driving mirror, she saw that her face was pale, her green eyes wide and shocked. The hands that had dropped to her lap were trembling. She did not want her grandfather to see her in this state, but if he had seen the car he would be waiting for her.

After several deliberately long breaths, she felt composed enough to leave the car and make her way to the cottage. Originally part of the estate, it was a small, white-walled house in which the High Valley farm supervisor had at one time made his home. With two bedrooms, smallish living-room and a kitchen that was not big enough to hold more than the most basic of modern domestic conveniences, the cottage was a far cry from the great gabled mansion which generations of Dubois had added to through the years. Nevertheless, it had its own appeal, which was why Grant Dubois had insisted on retaining it when he had sold the property. It was a comfortable little place, cool in summer, warm in winter, and so close to the boundaries of High Valley that the man who had centuries of Dubois blood in his veins could pretend to himself that he had not cut all ties with his former home.

Liane swung her bag over her shoulder, and walked quickly to the front of the cottage. She stopped still when she saw her grandfather. For once, he was not at the living-room window, watching for her car. He was outside today, on the *stoep*, sitting deep in a cushioned wicker chair, an old hat pushed backwards on his head, a gnarled hand absent-mindedly stroking the sleeping dog at his feet, his favourite pipe dropping ash on to his grey sweater. He was gazing across the fields of High Valley. Absorbed in his thoughts, he was not even aware of Liane at the bottom of the steps.

Something wrenched in her as she watched him. Every month Gramps seemed a little frailer and more dependent on her, so that it was almost impossible to remember the relentless, single-minded farmer he had been until just a few years ago, before adversity had changed him—the man who had given Kyle Avery and his father an hour to leave their home.

Grant Dubois—once he had been the owner of one of the biggest farms in the Cape—wealthy, successful, fiercely protective of his home, his estate, and his granddaughter. Liane had heard him called autocratic and merciless, and she knew the words to be accurate—though it was some time since they could have been applied to him—but she was devoted to him in spite of his failings. Her parents had died in a motor accident when she was very young. Gramps had taken her in, raised her, taken care of her, loved her—and yes, Kyle was right, he had cosseted her.

'Hello, Gramps.' Forcing the sadness from her tone, she walked quickly up the steps.

'Why, *liefie*!' He turned his head to look at her. 'I didn't hear you come.'

She bent to kiss the weather-roughened cheek. 'No wonder; I noticed your mind was far away.'

'Only as far as the fields beyond that fence.'

'I had an idea you were thinking about High Valley.'

'Hard to believe it will pass into other hands soon. You'll be giving all the keys to Martin Simpson tomorrow, I suppose?'

'Most of them.' Liane took a breath. 'Actually, I gave away the key to the front door of the house today.'

'Martin wanted to look around, did he?'

'Not exactly...' Liane hesitated. Gramps would have to know the truth sooner or later, and she wished she knew how he would take the news.

'So many generations of Dubois, farming the land, living in the house. If only I hadn't made that ridiculous investment, that incredibly stupid investment...' He seemed not to have noticed her evasiveness, his mind obviously back on the estate that had been his home. 'How could I have been so foolish, Liane? I'll never understand it.'

'Maybe not, but it's time you stopped blaming yourself, Gramps. People do make mistakes, and you had no way of knowing you'd lose so much money.'

'My father left the place to me, he had it from his father. Your father would have had it if he'd lived long enough.'

'Gramps, please——'

'I can't stop thinking about it, Liane. I think about it all the time. High Valley should have been yours. You should have raised your family there one day.'

But for a ghastly night seven years earlier the scenario he envisaged might well have taken place. Not that it would have given him any pleasure.

Briskly, and in an effort to divert his thoughts, Liane put down her bag, removed her jacket, then brushed the dry ashes from his sweater.

'When are you going to get rid of that disreputable old pipe?'

'Disreputable indeed!' he protested. 'Smoking is one of the few pleasures I have left to me.'

'I wouldn't mind so much if you were more careful. I keep worrying that you'll doze off with the pipe in your mouth.'

'Come now, Liane.'

'You could set yourself alight,' she pointed out.

'I wouldn't do anything so silly. Stop nagging, *liefie*, and tell me about your day.'

'Had a busy time at the winery.'

'Where you worked your butt off so that you could support your old grandfather in the manner in which he should be supporting you.'

'Determined to be cranky today, aren't you?' But she was smiling at him.

'Another of my few remaining pleasures. Besides, it's true, Liane. Without your earnings, we wouldn't be able to manage.' He saw the distress in her face and said, 'All right, all right, enough of that. Now tell me—what made you give Martin Simpson the key of the house a day early? Did you run into him at the office?'

Liane's eyes left her grandfather's face and went to the land beyond the fence. Hundreds of acres, stretching along the valley towards the blue-hazed mountains. Two hundred and fifty years ago a young man from France had seen this land, fallen in love with it, desired it, and made it his own. And now another man, desiring it too—though for a different reason, Liane speculated grimly—was about to settle there.

'I didn't give the key to Martin,' she said.

Something in her tone caught her grandfather's attention. He was watching her intently now.

'I went to High Valley,' she explained. 'I wanted to say my private goodbye to the house while I could.'

'Something tells me you met the new owners.'

'Owner. Just one person, Gramps. And yes, I met him.'

She lifted her head, her eyes bright with an emotion which her grandfather did not understand.

'*Well*?' He was sitting forward in his chair now. 'Who is this person? We never did get to know the purchaser's name.'

'You're not going to like this, Gramps.'

'Liane...?'

'But you do have to know all the same...'

'Don't keep me in suspense like this, *liefie*!'

'The man who bought High Valley is Kyle Avery.'

The old man in the wicker chair did not move. Not a flicker of expression crossed the weather-beaten face. He was so still that Liane wondered if he had heard her.

'I said Kyle Avery is the new owner of High Valley.'

'I heard you.'

'You remember Kyle, don't you?' Liane was staring at her grandfather, surprised by his lack of reaction.

'I remember him.'

'And that's all you have to say?'

'It's not all I have to say.'

Grant Dubois's body was suddenly rigid. His faded eyes blazed with the anger before which, in years gone by, countless men and not a few women had found themselves quaking. Liane had dreaded his reaction with good reason.

'Gramps——'

'I vividly remember a person called Kyle Avery, Liane. A lout. A swine.'

'Gramps, don't——'

'A selfish, unprincipled, ungrateful stable-hand who forced himself on to an innocent seventeen-year-old girl.'

'You've got it all wrong,' she whispered.

'He made you pregnant, didn't he?' her grandfather demanded.

'He didn't force himself on me.' Liane was trembling now.

'I could have called in the police, had him charged with rape.'

'It wasn't rape,' she insisted.

'That's what you say now.'

'It's the truth. And you shouldn't have thrown him out of High Valley. I didn't know about your part in his leaving until today.'

'Lucky for him that was all I did,' he growled.

'You shouldn't have done it, Gramps. I thought...' Liane's eyes clouded as she remembered the agonies she had suffered, waiting for Kyle to return, waiting for some word from him. 'I thought you'd told him about the pregnancy, and that he'd taken off because he couldn't handle the idea of being a father.'

'Are you mad, Liane? I wouldn't have told him you were pregnant—not in a million years! I threw him out because he'd been having sexual relations with my granddaughter.'

'Why didn't you tell him about the baby?'

'Think, *liefie*. A fellow like that—who knows what he'd have done if he'd known he'd fathered a Dubois child? He could have made unrealistic demands. Blackmailed us. Held us to ransom.'

'He wouldn't have done that. Not Kyle.'

At least, not the Kyle she had known then.

Liane found she was unable to look at her grandfather. Her eyes went back to the distant mountains.

'Kyle and I both wanted to make love,' she said softly. 'I was so much in love with him, Gramps.'

'Don't talk like that!' her grandfather burst out fiercely. 'I can't stand to hear such words coming from your lips!'

She turned back to him. 'I'm only telling you the truth. I know we haven't spoken of it in years, but that doesn't mean I haven't thought about it. About the baby. *Our baby*! About Kyle.'

'Liane——'

'To you he was only a stable-hand. To me he was so much more. No, Gramps, don't look at me like that! It's time we talked about it. Kyle was good-looking and exciting and so much fun. I was crazy about him.'

'Still crazy about him now, are you?' The fierceness in her grandfather's eyes had been replaced by a watchful shrewdness.

'I didn't say that.' Liane's voice was flat. 'I'm no longer seventeen, and Kyle is much older too. We've both changed, Kyle even more than me perhaps. He isn't the stable-hand you remember. I didn't ask him what he does, but it's obvious he's become successful.'

Her grandfather was silent for a moment. He knocked his pipe on the arm of his chair, scattering more ash on his clothes as well as on the floor.

'Did you tell him about the baby, Liane?' he asked at last.

'No.'

'Will you tell him?'

'I'm not sure. I don't know what to do.'

'May as well keep quiet about it at this stage,' Grant Dubois said gruffly. 'No concern of his.'

'You're wrong, Gramps. It was his concern then, and perhaps it still is now.'

'No, Liane.'

'The fact is, so much time has gone by, and his feelings for me are obviously no longer the same as they once were. I sense that he despises me. In fact, I doubt very much that Kyle Avery would be the least bit interested in anything I could tell him.'

CHAPTER TWO

A FEW days later, Liane was once again on her way home from work. Something tightened inside her as she rounded a bend and saw the long wooden fence of High Valley.

Though she had said her farewells to the house, there was one place which she had not revisited. She had to see that place before Kyle Avery took possession of the farm. It did not matter that she had already handed over all the keys; the barn had never been kept locked— chances were it would still be open now.

She drove through the stone gates and along the oak-lined way to the house. She looked around warily as she stopped the car, but the brick pad was empty, and the house still had that empty look too. If she was going to see the barn again, the time to do so was now.

Seven years had passed since she had walked this way last, yet every step of the path was familiar—the loose stones and the scrub and the interlocking branches of oleanders and a bougainvillaea. There was a reason why the barn had been such a wonderful meeting place: no casual observer would have spotted it behind the under-growth, and even those who knew of its existence seldom went there.

Paint was peeling away in long strips from the outer walls of the crumbling building, and cobwebs covered the door. Rusty hinges protested loudly as Liane pushed open the door, and a startled bird squawked as it fled from its chimney-pot nest.

She stood in the doorway, her nose wrinkling at the musty smell, her eyes straining to see in the dark. For a moment she was tempted to go back the way she had come, but this particular farewell was, in its way, even more important than the one she had said a few days earlier. And so she left the door and walked into the barn.

After a few moments her eyes grew accustomed to the dim light, and she walked further. She looked around her, seeing the old table and chairs, the ancient Primus stove where she and Kyle had boiled water for tea, the little chest where they had kept a few groceries, and suddenly she was flooded with memories.

She was touching a chair, her fingers making channels in the thick dust, when someone said, 'Perfect hideaway, wasn't it?'

Heart thudding in her throat, Liane spun around. '*Kyle*!'

'The ideal spot for lovers who didn't want to be seen.'

'You gave me an awful fright! What on earth are you doing here?'

'May I remind you that I own the place now?' retorted Kyle.

'But... You said it would be some time before you came here to live.'

'Do I have to account to you for my movements? I'm not the stable-hand any more, Liane.'

The light was behind him in the doorway, so that she could see his eyes mocking her. Her legs were so weak suddenly that she had to clutch the chair for support. Though Kyle was nowhere near her, she was intensely aware of his presence. She had banked on being alone in the barn, and now he was here, and invading her privacy in a way that made her feel at the same time excited and intensely nervous.

'I simply thought... Of course, you don't have to account to me...'

'You sound flustered,' he commented.

'I didn't expect to find you here, that's all.'

'Remember me saying I'd be seeing you around?'

'I didn't see your car...'

'I'm not here by car this time,' he told her. 'I flew in this morning from Johannesburg. Martin Simpson met me in Cape Town and gave me a lift back to High Valley.'

'And you just happened to take a little stroll down to the old barn.' Liane had begun to recover her composure. 'Stretching coincidence a bit far, isn't it, Kyle?'

'I agree. Actually, I was in the library when you arrived. I saw you drive up. I thought you were coming to the house, but you walked away from it, so I decided to join you.'

'You could have called out to me.'

'I could have, I suppose. I preferred not to.'

'You decided to follow me instead,' she accused.

'I waited a few minutes, then came this way.'

'You knew I'd be here.' Her voice shook.

'I thought you might be,' he agreed.

'What made you so sure?' she asked through dry lips.

Kyle took a step in her direction. 'I thought you might have some ghosts to lay,' he said then.

Liane swallowed hard. The fact that this harsh stranger understood the workings of her mind so completely was unnerving.

'You don't know that,' she said unsteadily.

'I think I'm right.'

'Kyle——' She was about to push past him.

'You see, Liane, I have ghosts too. And memories.'

The words, spoken so softly, stopped her.

'Memories of a young girl,' Kyle went on. 'She was so shy at first, so tremulous. Innocent and inexperienced—or so I thought.'

'Don't...'

'Yet passionate too. Passionate beyond anything I'd ever imagined. I remember being astonished by her ardour.'

'I wish you'd stop.' She was trembling.

'I was only a lowly stable-boy with no right to touch the precious granddaughter of Grant Dubois, but she seemed to want me to kiss her just as much as I wanted to kiss her.'

'I don't want to listen to this——'

'Do you ever think back to the things we did here, Liane?' His tone was still soft, yet utterly relentless.

'I've had enough!'

Liane made for the doorway. The problem was that in order to leave the barn she had to pass Kyle. His hands were ready for her. Hardly moving from where he stood, he reached for her, seizing her arm, preventing her from going further.

'You're not going to keep me here against my will, are you?' she demanded.

'Of course not. I never did anything against your will, Liane. I never forced you to do a thing you didn't want to do too.'

Liane was glad it was too dark in the barn for Kyle to see her flushed face. 'That's true,' she said, 'you didn't force me—not then. But you're holding me here now, when you know I want to go.'

'I'll let you go when you've answered my question.'

She moved restlessly. She was wearing a sleeveless summer dress, and his fingers were separate shafts of fire on her bare skin. 'What question was that?'

'Do you ever think back to what we did here together?'

'Seven years,' she said harshly. 'That's a long time, Kyle. We were kids.'

'I wasn't a kid, I was twenty-three. And even if you were only seventeen you were already a young woman.'

'Maybe. But Kyle, we're no longer the people we were then.'

The fingers on her arm tightened. He was so close to her that the clean smell of his aftershave rose above the mustiness of the air. Deep inside Liane a longing stirred, aching, hungry, crying for fulfilment—the longing of a mature woman this time, for a pleasure she had known once, in a world which no longer existed.

'*Do you think of it?*' The urgency in his fingers was in his tone now as well.

'Sometimes,' Liane admitted, her voice low.

'I wouldn't have believed you if you'd said you didn't.'

Abruptly, Kyle's hand left her arm. He walked further into the barn, stopping beside the chair Liane had touched. She could have left the barn now, but something kept her rooted to the spot. She watched him touch the chairs, the table, watched him open the box. Something dropped to the ground. Kyle picked it up and looked at it.

'A biscuit!' There was laughter in his voice. 'Stone-hard by now. I'm surprised the mice didn't get to it long ago.'

'I expect they polished off anything else we might have left here.'

'I expect they did. We did more than make love here, Liane. Remember the fun we had?'

Without thinking, Liane left the security of the doorway and walked closer to Kyle. 'We did have a good time,' she said. 'I took a chance scrounging the chairs and the table from the house. And the food. The strange thing was, nothing was ever missed. The housekeeper wondered sometimes why I'd suddenly developed such an appetite, but I don't think she was ever suspicious.'

Kyle laughed again. 'Dad wondered where I was carting all that hay, but he wasn't suspicious either.'

Liane smiled. 'We were like two children playing house.'

'For me the best part was being alone with you. Kissing you, making love to you.'

'We only went all the way twice,' Liane said on a tight throat.

'The end was unexpected.' The laughter had vanished from Kyle's voice now.

'Yes...'

'How did your grandfather find out about us, Liane? I can't believe you'd have told him.'

'I didn't.'

'Did he follow us here?'

The memories were still so painful that it was an effort to speak. 'No... He didn't follow us.'

'Someone must have told him.'

'Someone did,' she whispered.

'Who?'

'It isn't important, Kyle. Not any more.'

'*Who*?' he insisted. 'Nobody knew about us—at least, not to my knowledge.'

'I don't want to talk about it.'

'I do,' he insisted.

For a few minutes, forgetting that the carefree young man she had once adored had turned into a hard and unforgiving stranger, Liane had allowed herself to relax her guard. She shouldn't have done that, she realised now. She stepped away from him.

'I have to go,' she said.

'Not so fast.' Once more, without warning, he took hold of her.

Liane tried to still her trembling. 'There's nothing I can tell you.'

In the darkness she sensed him staring down at her, could feel his eyes boring deep into hers.

'I think you're lying, and I don't know why.'

'Kyle, please...'

'Tell me this at least, Liane. After your grandfather threw me out, did you continue to come here to the barn?'

'What does it matter?'

'It matters.' There was fierceness in his tone. 'Did you come here, Liane? Did you go on with someone else where you left off with me?' Every word was hard, biting, searing.

'How dare you?' she cried.

'Well—did you?'

'I came once,' she said painfully.

'Once? In all the years—only once?'

'Yes.'

'Why? For what purpose?'

'That's my business.'

Liane turned her head away as her eyes flooded with tears that were impossible to suppress. Every second of that last night in the dark barn was vividly raw in her mind. But there were things she was not yet ready to tell this new Kyle, even if he did have some right to know them.

She doubted that she could talk without weeping about the night when she had slipped on a patch of oil in the kitchen, struck her head hard against a counter, and fallen to the floor unconscious. Her grandfather had rushed her to hospital. There, for the first time, they had both learned that she was pregnant. That same night, she understood now, an enraged Grant Dubois must have dashed home and ejected Kyle and his father from the farm.

A few days after the fall in the kitchen, Liane had lost her baby. Back at the farm two days after the miscarriage, she had been greeted by a new stable-hand. Kyle was gone, the lad had informed her, a fact later confirmed by her grim-faced grandfather. No amount of tears had elicited any information as to where Kyle had gone or where she could find him.

Late that night, when the house was dark and silent, she had crept through the side-door with a flashlight, and had paid her last visit to the barn. The sights and smells that had greeted her there were familiar, only this time there had been no laughing Kyle to put his arms around her and kiss her until she was half crazy with love for him.

Alone in the darkness, curled up on the bed of hay Kyle had made for them, Liane had wept until there were no tears left.

'Liane,' Kyle said softly.

'Yes?' Her head was still averted.

'What's wrong?'

'Nothing.'

'You forget—I know you so well. You're upset.'

She did not answer him.

'Why are you crying?'

'I'm not...'

'Look at me,' he ordered.

'Just let me go,' she whispered in a strangled voice.

She flinched when he touched her face, his fingers on her eyelids, and then on the soft skin beneath her lashes.

'I thought you were crying.'

'Damn you, Kyle! Don't you have the tact to know when to stop?'

'Why?' he asked, as if he hadn't heard her.

It was clear that he would not release her until she had given him a reason for her tears. She could not tell him about the baby—not now, anyway. But she had to say something.

'You said yourself there were memories.' She forced herself to look at him. 'I was seventeen when we came here together. And you were right, Kyle, I was innocent until then. A girl's first sexual experience has to mean something to her.'

'*First*? Then there have been others?'

'I'm twenty-four, and now you're overstepping the limits.' She tried to move away from him. 'Let me go now.'

'There's one thing I want to do first.'

His voice, deliberately sensuous, told her what was coming even before he reached for her and drew her into his arms. There might have been a moment when she could have escaped him, but she was not quick enough to seize it—and perhaps she was just vulnerable enough not to want to. As his mouth came down on hers, she closed her eyes.

In the first years after their enforced parting she had longed for Kyle so intensely that she had dreamed of him night after night. Reality merged with those dreams now, making them one. The kiss they had begun quite softly was growing harder, his lips were pushing against hers, demanding a response, and after a moment her lips parted. All the remembered sweetness was there, the insistence of his tongue, the taste of him, the way he held her head as they kissed, the way they *fitted* together as if made for each other. His hands began to move over her, one hand sliding up across her back to her throat, pushing beneath the fall of her hair to hold her neck in a way that was familiar too. In the grip of a hunger too long unfulfilled, Liane was robbed of all rational thought. Her arms went around Kyle's neck as she pressed her body against his and reciprocated his kisses.

When he lifted his head, she wrapped her arms even more closely around him, her body crying out with a need that had been dormant for too long.

'Well,' she heard him say, his voice so strange.

'Kyle...' She looked up at him, dazed.

'This is a lot more than I hoped for when I followed you to the barn.'

'What...what do you mean?'

'This, sweetheart.' He lifted her against him and began to carry her towards the corner where their bed of hay had once been.

'You don't really think——'

'We're going to make love, Liane. This is where it all started—isn't it fitting that it continue here?'

There was a strange bitterness in his tone, and it returned Liane to instant sanity. This man was not the Kyle she had once adored, the sweet, tender young man who had awakened her to womanhood with his passion. This was a hard, mocking stranger who despised her and hated her grandfather.

Suddenly she was struggling against him.

He laughed, his breath warm on her cheek. 'Patience, sweetheart. We're getting there.'

'Put me down!'

He did put her down, only pausing to place his jacket beneath her on the bit of old hay. And then he was bending over her, kissing her again as he began to undo the front buttons of her dress.

'*No*!' She was pushing hard against him with her fists.

He sat back on his heels. 'What's wrong now?'

'I have to get out of here!'

His eyes narrowed. 'Don't tell me I misread you.'

Liane did up her buttons with trembling fingers. 'I can't go on with this.'

'Moments ago you wanted it very badly—and don't try telling me otherwise.'

She touched her burning cheeks. 'I didn't know what I was doing... I was confused.'

'You were the eager, passionate girl of my memory.'

He bent towards her again, but this time she was ready for him. Pushing him away, she sat up. 'What happened just now—shouldn't have happened. I wish it hadn't.'

'But it did,' he said softly. 'So now I have to wonder why.'

'Put it down to temporary craziness. Don't read more into it than that,' she said harshly. 'The girl you remember no longer exists. If I'd known you were at High Valley, that there was the slightest chance you'd follow me, I'd never have come here.'

She stumbled out of the barn. Ignoring the loose stones, and the thorns and blackjacks that clung to her clothes, she ran along the path that led to the house. She did not look back once to see if Kyle was following her.

The car jerked in protest as she turned the key and slammed her foot down hard on the accelerator. The ageing Honda responded best to tender treatment, and normally Liane was careful how she drove, but the health of her car was far from her mind as she shot around the bends of the farm road. Only when she had left the stone gates of High Valley behind her, when the house itself was out of view, did she draw up on a sandy stretch beside the road.

In her stumbling rush from the barn, she had ignored the hay that clung to her clothes, but her grandfather would see the condition she was in and remark on it. It was getting quite late, the sky was awash with the brilliant colours of the sunset and the distant mountains were hazy and indistinct. Gramps would be wondering where she was, but for a few minutes she was unable to move. Sitting deep in her seat, she opened her window and took a few jerky gasps of air.

Eventually she began to pull at the hay and the thorns and the blackjacks, a cumbersome chore, for the stuff had become embedded in the light jersey-knit fabric of her dress. When she had removed the last of it from her clothes and brushed it out of the car, Liane leaned forward and studied herself in the driving mirror.

The sight of her face dismayed her. Her auburn hair was a mess, but that was easily repaired with the comb she always kept in her bag. Harder to do something about were her eyes, which were wild and wide and shocked. Her grandfather would take one look at her eyes and know that something had happened. Grimly Liane opened the cubby-hole and took out her sunglasses. At worst, Gramps would joke about the fact that she was so preoccupied that she had forgotten to take off her glasses when she'd come out of the sun. If he were to know the truth about Kyle and what had just happened, his fury would have no limits.

Two weeks went by. As she passed High Valley on her way to and from work every day, Liane's eyes would go to the high gable of the beautiful farmhouse nestled in the trees some distance from the road. Had Kyle already taken up residence there? There was an easy way to find out, but she had no intention of visiting the estate again.

Late one Friday afternoon, she took a sip from the cool drink her grandfather had had waiting for her on her return home from work, then leaned back in her chair. The wine industry was undergoing certain changes, with the result that she had had to put in many hours of overtime at the office all week, and now she was looking forward to two days of complete relaxation. Closing her eyes, she let herself enjoy the sounds and the smells of summer: the scent of newly mown grass, the heady perfume of the jasmine that surrounded the house, the buzzing of bees on the Iceland poppies beside the *stoep*.

Half asleep, she did not hear the soft sound of wheels on the dirt road.

'A car just drove up,' said her grandfather.

'Expecting someone, Gramps?'

'Only Hester Downs with the eggs, but she doesn't have a silver car.'

'*Silver*?' Liane's eyes snapped open, and she jerked upright in her chair.

'I wonder who it can be, *liefie*?'

Grant Dubois was standing by the low brick wall of the *stoep*, his expression puzzled as he looked in the direction of the car.

Liane stood up abruptly, straightening her clothes and running an agitated hand over her hair. 'If I'm not mistaken, it's our new neighbour come to pay us a visit.'

'The stable-boy?'

'His name is Kyle Avery, and it's a long time since he was a stable-boy. I think you'd better remember that, Gramps.'

'To me he will always be the scum-bag who got you into trouble.'

'Not a word of that to Kyle,' Liane said in alarm. 'And Gramps, please, be friendly to him.'

'You don't know what you're asking.' The old man's lips were tightly set.

'At least make an effort to be civil. If the two of you start your new relationship on a bad footing, life here will be a nightmare.'

'I won't promise anything,' grumbled Grant Dubois. '*If* I'm civil—and, I warn you, the fellow had better be civil in return—I'd only make the effort for your sake, Liane. If it was up to me, I'd tell him to get the hell off my property and never show his face here again.'

'Here he comes,' Liane said softly.

Something moved inside her as Kyle came along the path towards the cottage. She was appalled at the fact that the mere sight of him, and the memory of their kisses, could send desire flooding through her, making her feel weak.

Every inch of the new Kyle exuded power and strength. Tan cords and a cream T-shirt clung to his body, revealing the muscles in his arms and chest. He had an easy, loose-limbed walk, the walk of a confident man who believed in himself. His hair had blown in the wind, and as he approached the *stoep* he brushed it back with his hand. Glancing at her grandfather, Liane caught a look of surprise in his eyes. Despite himself, Gramps was impressed.

Kyle threw Liane a smile from eyes that were warm and dark and amused—almost as if he guessed at the emotions that struggled within her—then he looked at her grandfather.

'Hello, Mr Dubois,' he said politely, and held out his hand.

Grant Dubois did not respond. Liane saw that his blue-veined hands were clenched tightly at his sides.

'Mr Dubois,' Kyle said again. His hand was still outstretched. On another man the gesture might have looked pathetic, a vain searching for a friendship that could never be attained; on Kyle Avery it was an invitation not to be refused with impunity.

Tensely, Liane looked from the dry, clenched right hand of the one man to the strong, long-fingered hand of the other.

'Gramps,' she whispered very softly.

'Why are you here?' muttered her grandfather.

'We're neighbours now.'

'I would never have sold High Valley if I'd known you were the buyer.'

'But you did sell. And we *are* neighbours. Are you going to shake my hand, Mr Dubois?'

Slowly, very slowly, as if the movement required superhuman physical effort, Grant Dubois' right hand unclenched, lifted—and met Kyle's hand.

Liane exhaled a breath she had not known she was holding. 'Why don't you both sit down and I'll get us something to drink?' she suggested in a brittle voice.

'Sounds like a good idea,' Kyle said.

Grant Dubois muttered, 'There's beer in the fridge.' His tone was far from gracious, but Liane knew that her grandfather had forced himself to accept a situation he had no choice but to accept.

She left the *stoep* and went into the house. She did not go directly to the kitchen, but went to the bathroom instead. Grimly she glanced in the mirror. Then she splashed her face with cool water, ran a brush through her hair, and applied a touch of lip-gloss. She would have liked to change into something more flattering than the old jeans and blouse she had thrown on after her return from the winery, but a change of clothes would give Kyle a sense of importance and power which he did not deserve.

In the kitchen, she arranged a tray—a beer for each of the men, another orange juice for herself. She was fond of beer too, but even a small amount of alcohol sometimes affected her adversely, and in any exchange with Kyle Avery she knew she needed a clear head.

Returning to the *stoep*, she found both men seated. They had been talking, but her arrival brought both heads turning her way.

When she had given them their beers, her grandfather said, 'I was just asking Kyle how he came by enough money to buy the estate.'

Liane, who had been wondering the same thing, said faintly, 'That's not a very polite question, Gramps.'

'But natural, in view of the fact that I left here a penniless stable-boy,' Kyle said, and she saw the grin that lit his eyes. 'You could say that by forcing me out of High Valley, Mr Dubois, you did me a good turn. If I'd remained here I'd probably still be working in the stables. As it is, I'm now the owner of quite a successful company. We manufacture farm implements. One of the things we make is a machine I invented, and I'm pleased to say it's selling well.'

'How about that?' Grant Dubois was unable to hide his surprise. 'And what do you plan to do at High Valley?'

Liane saw Kyle glance at the fields beyond the fence.

'I have certain plans,' he said. Putting down his mug, he got to his feet. 'I have to go. I enjoyed the beer, Liane, thank you.'

He held out his hand to Grant Dubois, and this time the old man did not hesitate to shake it.

'Goodbye, Kyle,' Liane said.

'I'd hoped you'd walk me to my car.'

'Yes, all right,' she agreed, after a moment.

She did not look at Kyle as they walked away from the cottage, but she was aware all the same of the long, lean body so close to hers. Once his arm brushed against her, and she had to make an effort to ignore the tingling sensation the touch provoked.

She waited until they were out of earshot. 'I have something to say to you,' she said then.

He grinned down at her. 'You want to arrange another meeting in the barn.'

'Don't be ridiculous!' she snapped.

'Is it ridiculous?' he drawled. 'I had the impression that you were enjoying every moment of what we did together—until you let yourself think about it. And then you decided you shouldn't be doing it.'

Liane lifted furious eyes. 'You enjoy humiliating me, don't you, Kyle? Just as you enjoyed humiliating my grandfather today. That was the purpose of your visit, wasn't it?'

'You don't believe I came out of a sense of good neighbourliness?'

'To see the man you hate? No, I don't believe that. Not for a second! I saw your eyes when Gramps asked you about your plans, and you didn't give him an answer.'

'You've become a perceptive woman, haven't you?'

'Whatever your plans are, I beg you to consider my grandfather.'

'Give me one good reason why I should do that.'

'Because I love him,' Liane said in a low voice.

'And you think I should love him too?' he mocked.

'That would be unrealistic, I know. I just want you to consider him.'

'Consideration for Grant Dubois... I remember every word the old devil said when he threw me out.' Kyle had a sombre look now. 'He told me that if I had any thoughts of marrying you I could think again. I'd never have his precious granddaughter, and I'd never lay my hands on the estate which you would one day inherit.'

Liane had begun to tremble. 'That was a long time ago. I'm surprised you still think about it.'

'Are you? Seven years, Liane, and his words stayed with me. On the day we left High Valley, my father in tears, our possessions hastily shoved into a few bags, I made up my mind that I would return. And not as the stable-hand.' Kyle looked at her with cold eyes. 'But I told you that the other day.'

'Yes, you did...' Liane was frightened, without quite knowing why. 'I understand what you've done by coming back here. You wanted to revenge yourself on my grandfather. Well, you have the estate now, Kyle. You have what you want.'

'Half of what I want,' he said lazily.

Liane took a step away from him. 'I don't understand...'

'I don't have the granddaughter.'

'What do you mean?' A shudder went through her. Despite the heat of the afternoon, she felt suddenly very cold.

His eyes held hers. 'I want you to be my wife.'

'You're crazy!'

'Not at all.'

'Why would you want to marry me?'

'Why does any man want to get married?'

'That's not the correct response in your case. Anyway, I know the reason. You want to complete your revenge. Because that's all it would be—revenge. It's obvious you don't love me, or you'd have been back a long time ago.'

'You haven't given me your answer.' Kyle was looking down at her, his eyes hooded, his expression enigmatic. 'Will you marry me?'

'Forget it!' Liane said, with a fierce shake of her head. 'The idea of marriage is ridiculous. It will never happen.'

'You wanted it once,' said Kyle, quite softly. 'Remember the times in the barn, when we dreamed and planned? You said you'd marry me when you were older.'

'We were kids then—I was, anyway. I had no idea what I was saying. Nor did you.'

He closed the gap between them, and gripped her shoulders in his hands. She had to stop herself flinching.

'We're adults now, Liane. I suggest you think about it.'

She jerked out of his hold. 'I don't need to. Whatever there may have been between us once doesn't exist any more—what happened the other day notwithstanding. You achieved the first part of your revenge, Kyle, by going through someone else. There's no way you'll ever achieve the second part.'

CHAPTER THREE

'THERE'S someone to see you, Liane.'

Liane looked up from her desk. She was well respected in the company, but for some reason her concentration had been well below par the last week, with the result that she was behind with her work. The 'out' basket held at least fifteen urgent letters waiting to be signed, and the 'in' basket was filled with Press releases, documents and correspondence requiring her urgent attention. Five telephone calls were still unanswered, and a long letter was just coming in on the fax machine.

She looked at the receptionist with a harassed expression. 'I'm sorry, Pat, but I'm up to my ears in work. I don't have time to see anyone today.'

'He's most insistent.'

'He doesn't have an appointment,' Liane said, glancing down at her desk diary.

'I know. I asked him about that, but he said he has to see you anyway.'

'Who is he, Pat?'

'I've no idea.'

The receptionist, fresh out of college, was willing, friendly and eager to learn, and Liane was fond of her. Hiding her impatience, she said, 'Surely he must have told you his name?'

'No—though I did ask him. He just said he had to see you.'

'Tell him it isn't possible. Be firm with him, Pat—polite, but really firm. I know it's not easy, but you're in the working world now, and you have to learn how to deal with all sorts of undesirable people.'

'This guy isn't an undesirable, Liane. He's very handsome—dynamite, in fact,' said Pat. 'One of those rugged outdoor types, with dark hair and high cheekbones.'

Rugged, with dark hair and high cheekbones... A face and a name came instantly to Liane's mind. For the first time she noticed the star-struck expression in the receptionist's eyes.

'Now, Pat...' she began.

'Don't you want to take a look at him, at least?'

'I guess I'll have to have a word with him,' Liane said, with a grimness that had the young girl puzzled. 'A brief word—no, not here in my office. Tell him I'll be out, but he'll have to wait a few minutes.'

When Pat had left the office, Liane crossed the floor to the fax machine and read the letter which had just come in. It concerned a wine festival, and required a prompt response, but when she sat down in her chair and lifted her pen the necessary words escaped her.

'Damn you, Kyle Avery!' she muttered. 'Do you have to intrude into this part of my life as well?'

The reception area of the winery was elegantly furnished in muted tones of grey and purple. Tapestry-upholstered chairs were arranged around mahogany tables, and pictures by well-known South African artists adorned the walls. Sitting on a chair that looked much too delicate for his long, strong body was Kyle.

Liane advanced on him without a smile. 'You can't just barge in here and demand to see me. What are you doing here anyway, Kyle?'

He smiled at her, his eyes alight with mischief. 'Really nice to see you too, Liane.'

'You haven't answered my question.'

He stood up. 'I'm taking you out for lunch.'

'I don't remember agreeing to go anywhere with you. Nor do I remember being invited.'

'We stand on ceremony now, do we? OK, we'll do it your way. Will you have lunch with me, my dear Miss Dubois?'

'No, Kyle, I won't. Now will you leave?'

'No.'

Liane looked over her shoulder at the receptionist, who was watching the scene with undisguised curiosity. Quietly, making certain she could not be overheard, she said, 'Do you have to be so stubborn?'

'I've asked you to have lunch with me. That isn't a major issue, is it? Unless, of course, you already have another more attractive engagement?'

'No...'

'Then you might as well come with me, Liane.'

She did not know whether to be exasperated or amused by his persistence. 'Do you always hold out for what you want, Kyle?'

'Every time,' he said pleasantly. 'I thought you knew that by now.'

'You made up your mind to own High Valley, and you succeeded.'

'Correct.'

'On the other hand, you will never...' She stopped. Her cheeks were suddenly flushed.

'"Never" is a word that doesn't exist in my vocabulary.' His eyes lingered on her face, taking in her embarrassment.

'But it does exist in mine. Please go, Kyle.'

'We'll go together.'

'What does it take to get through to you? I can't have lunch with you—can't you accept that?'

'It's a few minutes to one,' he said reasonably. 'In the time that I've been waiting here, I've seen most of your co-workers leave the office.'

'You have absolutely no idea how busy I am. There are two letters I should have answered half an hour ago, a million others that have to be attended to before the end of the day.'

'Even the busiest people have to eat.'

Two men walked by; one was the president of the winery, the other a wealthy buyer. Liane was aware of the looks they gave her and Kyle as they passed.

'This isn't fair, Kyle, you really are embarrassing me,' she said in a low voice.

'Will you come, Liane?'

It was clear that he would not leave unless she went with him, and equally clear that if she remained at her desk through the lunch-hour she would not put in five minutes' worth of productive work.

'Under duress,' she murmured crossly.

Kyle laughed, the sound low and vital and attractive. 'Better than nothing.'

'And I have to be back here on the dot of two.'

He laughed again. 'The sooner we go, the sooner you'll be back.'

He had made a reservation at a trendy Italian restaurant. Liane could not help being impressed as they were shown to a table at a window with a spectacular view towards the distant mountains.

'People are willing to part with huge bribes for this table,' she said. 'Did you twist the arm of the *maître d*'?'

Again that laugh. Liane felt it reaching inwards towards her heart, warming a piece that had been cold for too long.

'I have my ways of getting what I want,' he assured her.

'So I'm discovering.'

'The *maître d*' is a romantic Italian. When I told him I was lunching with a very beautiful lady, and that I'd been waiting years for the meal, he said, "*Mamma mia*, the lady must be special!" and gave me the table I asked for.'

It was difficult to remain angry with him, impossible to stop her eyes from dancing him a smile.

'I wish I were less susceptible to flattery,' she sighed. 'Why was it so important that I eat with you, Kyle?'

'I have a proposition for you.'

Liane tried to ignore the quickening beat of her pulse. 'I've already turned it down once.'

A dark eyebrow rose in amusement. 'That was a proposal, not a proposition. What makes you think I'd repeat it?'

'I...I thought that's what you were doing.'

'I'm not in the habit of pleading with women to marry me.'

She looked at him, her cheeks hot. 'I'm sorry... I guess I just assumed...'

'Wrongly, as it happens. I'll tell you about the proposition while we're eating. What will you have?'

She did not care what she ate; she wasn't in the least bit hungry, nor, at that moment, was she capable of making any kind of choice. Kyle's eyes were on her face. As if he understood her confusion, he picked up the menu, and ordered linguine with prawns for both of them. The wine steward arrived at the table, and Kyle requested a particularly good Cape Riesling.

'I still can't believe how much you've changed,' Liane said, after their meal had been put before them.

'Haven't you told me that already?'

'You've become so...' She searched for the right word.

'Worldly?' he supplied.

'I guess that would be it.'

'You think I'm worldly because I can charm a *maître d*' and order prawns and wine?'

She knew he was laughing at her again, but she said, 'That's part of it.'

'It doesn't mean very much, you know, Liane.'

'Maybe not. But everything taken together—your factory, all the things you've achieved ... I'm interested, Kyle. How did you get so far in such a short time?'

He shrugged. 'Luck.'

'I would think luck couldn't have played more than a tiny part in it. How *did* you do it, Kyle?'

'You're really interested?'

'I have been since the moment we met again.'

Dropping the banter, he talked to her then. He told her about his fierce determination to make something of himself. About the courses at night school, and afterwards at university. About the work he'd done at the same time as he studied—menial jobs at first, but a way of acquiring money for food and shelter. He told her about the engineering company where he'd started as an apprentice. About the money he had saved, and the investment he had made, a shrewd investment that had netted him enough for a down-payment on the company when the original owner, childless and ill, decided to retire. And he told her about the machine he'd invented, which was beginning to earn him a fortune.

Liane listened quietly as he talked, marvelling at all the things he was telling her. But she was watching him too—taking in the intelligent eyes, the sensuous mouth, the proud thrust of the head, the strong lines of his cheeks and jaw—and she thought how attractive he was. The young Kyle had had an appeal that she'd found irresistible. The older Kyle was—yes, Pat was right—dynamite.

After a while he glanced at his watch. 'You'll be wanting to get back to work soon.'

She felt as if she could sit all afternoon with him at the table by the window and never grow bored. 'I will have to leave,' she said, and wondered if he could hear the reluctance in her tone.

'Not before I tell you about my proposition, though.'

She looked at him expectantly.

'I want to throw a party at High Valley.'

'A party?' Liane was puzzled. Also a little let down. 'You took me out to lunch so that you could invite me to a party?'

'Not quite. It'll be a big party, Liane—grand. I have memories of other parties at High Valley. Dad would park the cars, and I would help him look after them. I used to watch the guests arrive, and I'd look at the lights and listen to the music. Once I crept up to the windows on the veranda—I wanted so badly to look inside—but Dad pulled me back. He was nervous I'd be seen; he was always worried I'd get into trouble.' His lips tightened. 'Even Dad didn't foresee the trouble I did get us into.'

'And now you're the owner of High Valley, and you want to have a party of your own,' Liane said softly.

'I want to get acquainted with my neighbours—with the owners of all the nearby farms, with the people whose cars my father used to park. He was always so glad of their tips.'

The hint of contempt in his voice had Liane swinging up her head. 'Why are you telling me all this?'

'I want you to be my hostess.'

'Are you serious?' She looked at him in astonishment.

'Perfectly.'

'Why?'

'Isn't it obvious?'

Liane looked at the rugged face, and forced herself not to think about the desire that was building inside her.

'It isn't obvious at all. I think you should explain, Kyle.'

'You'll be the ideal hostess,' he told her.

'Why?'

'You may be living in a cottage on the other side of the property fence, but you're still Liane Dubois.'

'You think my name will make a statement,' she said drily.

'I think you should know,' he said, his voice hard, 'that I'm discriminating about the people I break bread with on a regular basis. I have no time for fools or flatterers or snobs, and I don't need them as my friends. I don't give a damn who knows that I was a stable-hand. I'm not ashamed of what I was, Liane. At the same time, I want to get to know my neighbours and to associate with them on an equal footing.'

When it came to equality, Liane thought, there was not a man for a hundred miles around who could hold a candle to Kyle Avery and not be extinguished in the contest.

'It's important to me,' he said, 'that my children will one day be accepted by these people.'

'Your children?' She looked at him, startled. 'You don't even have a wife!'

'You could have been my wife, but you turned me down.'

'Do you have someone else in mind?' The question was out before she could stop it.

His eyes glittered. 'Let's just say that I don't intend to remain a bachelor all my life.'

And he did not make a habit of repeating his proposals. Liane took a sip of her wine, her fingers holding the slender stem of the glass more tightly than was necessary.

'Will you be my hostess?' Kyle asked.

'I don't know...'

'You have reservations?'

'I do, yes. Gramps and I have made a break with High Valley. A very painful break, Kyle. I don't know that it would be a good idea for me to go back there now as anything but a guest.'

Without warning, Kyle reached across the table and put his hand over one of hers. His palm was rough from all the years of hard physical labour; it was also warm and strong, and it made the feelings that ached within her intensify.

'Think of it,' he said. 'You could help me bring some vitality to High Valley. It's little more than a shell right now, Liane. I don't know why your grandfather neglected the place in the last years, but we both know that he did. Wouldn't you like to see that beautiful house come alive again?'

'Of course—but you don't need me for that, Kyle.'

'I do,' he said. 'I understand horses. I know about farm implements and machinery and making money, but I've never planned a party. I wouldn't know where to begin.'

'It isn't difficult. I'm sure you could do it.'

'Let's do it together.'

Liane swallowed hard for a second at the intimacy of the words.

'You don't know what you're asking,' she said then. 'High Valley isn't my home any more.'

'I believe part of your heart remained there when you left.' Kyle's hand tightened on hers. 'Can't you see it? The house alive and glowing, flowers in all the rooms, the reception area ablaze with light, musicians roving around, serenading the guests.'

She gave him a look of wry amusement. 'I understand now why the *maître d'* gave you this table. Obviously you painted him quite a picture.'

His thumb stroked her hand, sending ripples of sensation along her wrist and up her arm. 'More to the point, Liane, am I painting an inviting picture for you?'

'Yes...'

'Does it tempt you?'

Liane turned her eyes away from Kyle, and looked unseeingly across the crowded restaurant. Kyle was right when he said that the big house had become a shell, that her grandfather had neglected it. The investment which had lost Gramps his money had also deprived him of the opportunity to give High Valley the attention it deserved. It had hurt him greatly—had hurt them both—to see the dowdiness which had settled over the estate. And now here was Kyle Avery, with all the money and zest and enthusiasm that was necessary to make the house live once more. And—oh, yes!—Liane *could* see the lights and the flowers, *could* hear the music. And she wanted very much to be part of the transformation and the excitement.

'*Does* it tempt you?' Kyle asked again, softly.

'You know it does,' she said unsteadily.

'Then you'll be my hostess?'

'Yes.'

'Good.' Just that one word, but he sounded satisfied.

Suddenly Liane realised that his hand was still holding hers. She could not meet his eyes as she withdrew it. Instead, she glanced at her watch.

'Will you look at the time? I should have gone by now. We're not going to be able to do any party planning today, Kyle.'

'We'll start on that another day. Have lunch with me on Saturday.'

Liane hesitated. It was one thing to act as Kyle's party hostess, quite another to be thrust into the constant company of a man whose sexuality made her nerve-ends feel raw.

'I take it you mean a working lunch,' she said briskly.

Dark brows lifted in amusement. 'Of course. What else?'

'What time shall we meet, and where?' she asked.

'High Valley. Around noon.'

The thought of being all alone with Kyle in that big, empty house made her feel a little breathless. 'Why High Valley?'

'It's the obvious place.'

'Not necessarily. You could come over to the cottage, and I could make us all a snack. My grandfather wouldn't mind—he might even give us a few helpful suggestions.'

Gramps would also be an effective deterrent if Kyle had anything but party planning in mind.

'Thanks, but my preference is still High Valley. Considering it's the party venue, I think it's the ideal place to start our preparations.' His eyes held hers for a long moment. 'If it will make you feel any safer in my company, you can always bring along pen and paper,' he added insolently.

Beneath the checked tablecloth her fingers interlaced tightly. 'Pen and paper go without saying. And don't bother to pick me up—I'll make my own way.'

'Fine.' Kyle grinned at her for a moment, then he caught the waiter's eye and called for the bill.

Weekends were for sleeping late, but Liane woke up early that Saturday morning, and found Kyle's face behind her closed lids. A little grimly, she opened her eyes, pushed aside the blankets and got out of bed.

Quietly she left her room and went to the kitchen. When she had plugged in the kettle, she opened the door to the *stoep* and brought in the newspapers, glancing at the headlines until she heard the water boil. She made a pot of tea and carried a cup to her grandfather's room.

He sat up in bed. 'You're up early, *liefie*. Thinking of your date with that man, I suppose?'

'His name is Kyle, Gramps—I've told you that before. And it isn't a date. *He* certainly doesn't think of it in that way.'

'But you do.' The old man regarded her shrewdly. 'Look at you, Liane, you're as nervous as a child on the first day of school.'

'Maybe that's because I don't know if I did the right thing, agreeing to be Kyle's hostess.'

And that, she knew, was only partly the truth. She did have her doubts about the party, but they were only secondary to her reluctant anticipation at the thought of a day alone in Kyle's company.

'It's not too late to change your mind,' said her grandfather.

'I think it is. I said I'd do it. I can hardly let him down now.'

'You don't owe the man . . . Kyle . . . a damn thing.'

'That's not true, Gramps. I do owe him something, a great deal, in fact. You and I both know that I've done him a huge injustice.'

'Rubbish!' her grandfather said bluntly.

'I could have told him about the baby. Not at the time, of course, because he was no longer at High Valley when I got out of hospital. But I could have told him when I saw him again. I could still tell him.'

'You decided not to,' he pointed out.

'Because it's seven years too late, and until now there didn't seem to be a point.'

'There you are, then,' Grant Dubois said gruffly.

'Which doesn't make it right. But about the party . . . The fact is, I don't want to go back on my word. There's a part of me which will always think of High Valley as home, just as you do, Gramps. Kyle was right about that. If I don't agree to be his hostess, he'll find someone else and I really don't think I could bear that.'

'*Liefie*...' her grandfather had a troubled look '...I believe Kyle Avery could hurt you. I don't want to see that happen.'

'He can only hurt me if I let him. I wish you'd stop worrying about me, Gramps. I'm not seventeen any more. I'm twenty-four, and I know how to take care of myself.'

A little before noon, Liane left the cottage. She could have taken the car and gone by the road, but it was a lovely day, and she knew a short cut through the fields. This was a walk she loved. The early morning mist had long since lifted from the mountains...the great humped outlines were clear against the deep blue of the sky. It had rained during the night, washing the dust from a clump of eucalyptus trees, giving them a fresh look. Extending in one direction were vineyards, acre upon acre of grapes which would be made into fine Cape wine. Closer to the cottage was a biggish area which had been left uncultivated for some time. Liane wondered what plans Kyle had for this land.

Twenty minutes of fast walking brought her to the farmhouse. For the first time in months she was seeing it with the shutters pushed aside and the windows open. She was about to walk up the steps to the front door when she heard a chopping sound coming from the side of the house, and decided to walk in the direction of the sound.

Liane saw Kyle before he saw her. He was hewing wood, and she stood very still, filled with the need to watch him, unobserved, for as long as she could.

Gone was the sophisticated man who drove an expensive car and knew his way around haughty *maître d's* and choice wines. In his place was a man of the outdoors. Not the stable-hand of old, handsome and appealing, yet little more than a lad. Feet bare, wearing a pair of shabby shorts and a sleeveless T-shirt, this was a different person altogether. Kyle's body, deeply tanned, looked as hard as the tool that he was using. Corded muscles moved in his shoulders and arms, and his long thighs and calves were taut with effort. Liane watched as he raised the axe with both hands and swung it downwards, cleaving a log in two with one neat stroke.

She would have liked to go on watching him, but she had a sense of intruding on his privacy. On a dry throat, she said, 'Kyle...'

He turned, lowered the axe, and came towards her. 'Hello, I didn't realise you were here.' But the glint in his eyes told her that he guessed she'd been watching him.

'Not too early, I hope?' she asked.

He stopped in front of her, axe in one hand, the other hand on his hip. He exuded an animal sensuousness that was so intense that Liane thought if she tried she could touch it.

She took a step away from him. 'You look busy.'

His eyes sparkled. Not for the first time, Liane knew that he understood precisely the effect he had on her.

'I chopped some wood on our *braaivleis*. And then I decided to chop a little more for the fireplace in the living-room.'

'It's not winter yet,' she said.

'It isn't,' he agreed, 'but it's never too soon to start building a wood-pile. Will you share my fire with me sometimes, Liane?'

'Maybe...'

'We could make ourselves quite cosy. Shades of our old days together in the barn. We could have our meal by the fire, and later we'd——'

'*Don't*!' Liane exclaimed, her eyes closing involuntarily to shut out the picture he evoked.

Kyle took a tendril of her wind-blown hair and played with it in his fingers.

'Scared of me, Liane?' he asked lazily.

'Of course not!'

'You never used to be.'

'Don't flatter yourself, Kyle. I'm not scared of you now either.' But her voice was bumpy.

'Maybe,' he said, very softly, 'you're scared of yourself?'

It appalled her how close he was to the truth. With what ease she had assured her grandfather, just a little while earlier, that she could take care of herself. Now, with Kyle's closeness striking some primitive chord deep inside her, she wondered how she could have been so confident.

'I'm not a child any longer,' she said, instilling firmness into her voice. 'I'm not scared of anyone, least of all myself.'

Kyle looked down at her, his gaze on lips that trembled slightly, on eyes that couldn't hold his for more than a few seconds. He gave a soft laugh as he tucked her hair behind one ear.

'Time to eat,' he said.

Easily, as if it weighed nothing at all, he picked up one of the logs he had split, and Liane followed him to the brick barbecue at the back of the house.

She watched him start the fire, not surprised that he had the flames rising within minutes. When the fire had died low, Kyle fetched a tray of food from the house. He put two steaks on the grid, and *mielies* wrapped in foil. Then he opened two beers and handed one to Liane.

Grinning at her, he said, 'I haven't got round to buying garden furniture yet, but I didn't think you'd mind sitting on the grass. Kick off your shoes and make yourself comfortable. It'll be a while before the meat is ready.'

He joined her on the grass, leaning against a tree with his eyes closed. Liane watched him a few moments, but she was still feeling so unsettled that she made herself look in the direction of the cooking meat instead.

'My grandfather and I had so many meals out here,' she said, remembering.

The prone body on the grass was still.

'Didn't your father build the barbecue, Kyle?'

'He did.'

Just two words, but so grimly spoken that they had Liane jerking quickly upright. Looking at Kyle, she saw that though his eyes were still closed his lips had a tight and angry look.

In alarm, she said, 'I'm sorry, I didn't mean to offend you.'

'Offend? You're perfectly correct, my father built the barbecue. He loved working with his hands, and he was proud of what he did.'

'In that case, why do you sound so bitter?'

'All these years, have you ever given Dad a thought, Liane? Or was it out of sight, out of mind, the moment we were gone?'

'I . . .' She stopped.

'I don't need an answer. In fact, I prefer no answer at all to a dishonest one.'

'I always liked your father.' She felt helpless in the face of his bitterness.

'Did you? Did you really?'

'Kyle, I'm sorry. . . You don't know. . .' She stopped herself quickly. Even in the midst of her distress, she knew there were things that had to remain a secret.

Kyle was on his feet now, turning the meat on the grid. Liane saw the way the muscles bunched in his shoulders, and she knew that in his anger he had not heard her last words.

She stood up too. 'I think I should leave.'

'Don't go,' he said, without turning his head.

'I don't think I should stay.'

He turned back to her. His eyes were bleak. 'You can't help being born Liane Dubois.' He touched her face. 'Did you ever wonder how different things would have been if you hadn't been the granddaughter of Grant Dubois? We'd have been married long ago.'

'There's no point in this,' she said painfully.

'Don't go, Liane.'

'I think I should.'

'I still want you to be my hostess,' he said softly.

'It's no good, Kyle. There's too much bitterness between us.'

'There's still going to be a party.' He took her hand, turned it in his, touched her palm with the tip of his tongue, and all the while he held her eyes with his. 'The fact is, you're Liane Dubois, and you'll be the ideal hostess.'

Liane's hand was on fire, a fire that raced through her wrist and up her arm. Swallowing hard, she withdrew her hand from his, and forced it down to her side.

'Will you do it?' he persisted. 'Will you still be my hostess?'

There was a part of Liane which told her to walk away from Kyle. To leave High Valley, and never go there again. To forget what the place had meant to her family. Most of all, to forget what Kyle Avery had once meant to her. But his eyes were still on hers, seductive eyes, hard to resist.

'Yes, all right,' she muttered. 'I just hope I won't regret it.'

CHAPTER FOUR

'THE party,' Liane said matter-of-factly, when they had finished eating.

Kyle laughed. 'We've barely had time to digest our meal. Are you always so industrious?'

He was sitting back against the tree once more, relaxed now, as if he had forgotten the few moments of bitterness.

'This was meant to be a working lunch,' she reminded him.

'It was, wasn't it?' he agreed.

'Besides, I like to get things done.' In her own ears, the words sounded inane.

He stretched out a leg, prodding her thigh with a bare toe. 'I can see why you'd be invaluable to the winery.'

'I do what I have to.' She forced herself to ignore the probing toe. 'Now, about the party——'

'You were always such fun to be with, Liane.'

'Meaning I'm not any longer?'

'Meaning you could be—if you'd just let yourself go.'

The wicked toe was doing strange things to her. Restlessly, she moved beyond its reach.

'Seven years ago things were different. We were friends, Kyle. All right,' she admitted as she caught his sardonic eye, 'more than friends.'

Seven years ago she could not have imagined how terrible it could be to lose the man she loved, as well as the child they had conceived together.

'Are you saying we're not friends now?' His eyes were moving over her in a way that unnerved her.

'Need you ask, when you've made it clear that you despise me and hate my grandfather? That's hardly a basis for friendship.'

'I asked you to marry me,' he said levelly.

'Only because marriage would complete your revenge.'

'You know all my motives, of course.' The dark eyes were hooded now.

'You've made no secret of how you feel, Kyle,' Liane said firmly. 'We had a...a special relationship once, but it doesn't exist any longer.' Reaching for her bag, she took out a writing-pad and a pen. 'You invited me here to discuss the party, and I think we should do that. Where shall we start?'

'You tell me.' Kyle picked a long blade of grass and stroked it across the soft inner skin of her arm.

Liane kept her eyes on the paper in front of her. 'All right, then, how many people are you expecting?'

'You'll have to tell me that too.'

Her head jerked up. 'I don't believe this! I may be your hostess, but this is still *your* party, Kyle. You must know how many there'll be.'

'I don't even know who to invite,' he said lazily.

'This is ridiculous!'

He sat forward, and all at once the lazy teasing was gone from his eyes. 'I've told you the reason for this party, Liane. I want to get to know my neighbours. I don't give a damn if they never become my friends, but I need to know my children will be accepted.'

That word again. Children. Obviously, Kyle had marriage on his mind. If not to Liane—and he was not likely to repeat the offer she had already refused—then to whom?

'As a farm-hand I hardly became acquainted with the local social set,' he went on. 'So now I have to rely on you to help me out with the guest list.'

'You're really quite serious about this, aren't you?' Liane looked at him curiously.

'Of course.'

'How big do you want the party to be?'

'As big as it has to be.' He paused a moment. And then, his tone different, he asked, 'Do you think people will come?'

Liane was touched by the question. It was the first sign of vulnerability she had glimpsed in Kyle since his return.

'They'll come,' she said. 'Everyone's eager to meet the new owner of High Valley. I've heard them talk— in town and at the winery. Who is this Kyle Avery? they're all asking. What will he do with the farm? Is he young? Rich? Is he...?' She stopped.

'Am I what?' he prompted.

'It really isn't important.'

'You may as well finish the sentence.'

'Married.'

'Well.' There was a glint in his eyes.

'You can expect a certain amount of matchmaking,' she told him.

'It takes two to make a match, Liane.'

'So it does.' She looked down at her writing-pad. 'Well, shall we begin?'

'Miss Efficiency.' She heard his laughter as she wrote the words 'GUEST LIST' at the top of the first blank page, and the bare toe touched her again.

Refusing to look at him, she said, 'Let's begin with your nearest neighbours—the Fouries. The Bryants. Ian and Maria Taylor.'

'The names are vaguely familiar,' he mused.

'I'm sure they must be. They've all lived around here for as long as I can remember.'

'Wasn't there a couple with an old Bentley? Dark green and rather ancient?'

Liane laughed. 'So ancient that it would be a lot safer in a museum than on the roads. You're thinking of the Wileys. And yes, they're still driving that car.'

'And then there was a woman with flowing dresses and an ostrich-feather hat, who never travelled in anything but a horse-drawn buggy.'

'Hazel Marais. The horses have changed over the years, but she still wears the same clothes. Hazel adores a party; I know she'll want to come.'

'And a girl about your age, Liane. Elizabeth—Elise. No, that's not quite right, is it?'

'Elsbeth.' A frown-line appeared between Liane's fine-drawn eyebrows. 'Elsbeth Barber.'

'Mad about horses, wasn't she? She was always hanging around the stables.'

Elsbeth, as superficial as she was golden-haired and pretty, had never been particularly fond of horses. What she had had was a crush on Kyle, Liane remembered. The two girls had never been more than classroom acquaintances, but Elsbeth had had a way of inviting herself to High Valley. Never a visit that she had not found an excuse to go to the stables. To Liane, Elsbeth's interest in Kyle had seemed blatant, but at the time Liane and Kyle had been so crazy about each other that she had been merely amused by the other girl's manoeuvrings.

'Does she still live around here?' asked Kyle.

'Yes,' Liane said, and wondered whether Kyle had noticed her momentary hesitation.

In fact, Elsbeth, recently divorced, had returned to the Cape after three years of married life in the Transvaal. Liane had run into her on the street just a few weeks earlier, and had been struck by the other woman's brittle glamour.

'Add her to the list,' Kyle said.

Telling herself that she did not care who came to the party, Liane did so.

'Who else?' Kyle asked.

Liane mentioned other names, and they too were added to the list.

When she had jotted down more than forty names, she said, 'That's it. I can't think of anyone else.'

'There's one person we've left out.'

She looked up. 'Who?'

The stalk of grass tickled her bare arm. 'The man who, some might say, should have been at the head of the list.'

Liane was tense suddenly.

'We can't leave out your grandfather, master of High Valley for more years than most people can remember. The party wouldn't be complete without him.'

'It might not be wise...'

'I don't agree.'

Liane shifted her position on the grass. 'Gramps won't expect an invitation,' she said at last.

'That's a tactful way of saying you don't think he'll accept.'

'I didn't say that.'

'You didn't have to.' There was something autocratic in the lifting of Kyle's eyebrows. 'It's your grandfather's privilege to decline the invitation, but I want him invited anyway.'

'Kyle...'

'It's the way I want it, Liane.'

She looked at him uncertainly, seeing the confidence in his eyes, the firmness of his lips and jaw. In the years away from High Valley Kyle Avery had grown accustomed to having the upper hand in any situation.

She looked away from him, and back at the pad in front of her. And then, slowly, she added her grandfather's name to the bottom of the list.

With the guest list compiled, Liane wanted to proceed to other matters—food, flowers, music and wine.

'Oh, I don't think so,' Kyle said lazily.

She looked at him in surprise. 'I must have misunderstood. I thought you wanted my help with the whole party. I didn't realise you only needed me for the guest list.'

'You didn't misunderstand, Liane. You're not only going to be my hostess, I want your input and advice on everything I do.'

'And yet you don't want to talk about food.'

'Sure I do—but another time. No need to settle everything in one day. We'll meet again one evening during the week. I'll pick you up after work, and we'll have dinner together. We'll talk more about the party then.'

He was grinning at her, lips parted to reveal strong white teeth, dark eyes sparkling, and suddenly her heart was racing. He was so vital, so attractive, so incredibly sexy. It was no use telling herself that this was not the Kyle she had once known. She had never stopped yearning for the old Kyle, and she wanted this new Kyle even more now. She also knew that he could break her heart all over again. Last time it had not been his fault; this time he might do it deliberately.

'I'm not sure it's a good idea to discuss all the arrangements over dinner,' she said, a little breathlessly.

'I disagree.'

'Well, if we're not going to talk any more today, I may as well go home.'

'I still need your help.' Suddenly he was on his feet. Reaching for her hands, he pulled her up too. 'Let's go inside the house.'

It was absurd that his nearness should create havoc inside her—but there it was; all at once she felt intensely vulnerable.

She took her hands from his, and moved a step away from him. 'Why?' she asked coolly.

'The house needs repairs. Renovations.'

'I told you it did.'

'You can show me what has to be done.'

She shrugged. 'It's your home now, Kyle. I don't think it'll take you long to figure out what needs doing.'

'You know the place so much better than I do,' he said pleasantly. 'I'd welcome your suggestions.' His hands went to her face, tracing a feather-light path around her eyes, her lips. 'Explore with me. Please?'

It was impossible to refuse him.

'I'm not sure why I end up saying yes to you every time,' she said crossly.

'Every time?' he murmured seductively.

'A figure of speech. Don't make too much of it.'

His low laughter unnerved her. 'Come,' he said, and led her to the front of the house.

It was a strange feeling to watch Kyle fit the key with its ornamental head into the lock of the big wooden door, strange to walk into the house with him. He had taken her hand again, and she did not have the strength—or the will—to withdraw it from him. Together they walked from one room to another, and now Liane was seeing the house that had been her home for most of her life with the eyes of someone who was still fairly new to it. The big entrance hall, the living-room, with its yellow-wood floors and high, narrow windows, the dining-room, large enough to seat a family of twenty with ease, and the kitchen, with its pale cream walls and tiled floors. For the first time she was also seeing the full extent of the shabbiness which had come upon the house with the years.

'I knew we'd let things slide, but I hadn't realised quite how bad it had become.' Her tone was apologetic.

She looked up and saw Kyle watching her.

'You can grow so used to a place that you don't always notice the things that need doing,' she said defensively.

'From what I've heard, your grandfather stopped doing repairs some time ago.'

'That's true. Perhaps there were things he could have done, but somehow...' She paused, unwilling to put down the old man who had given her so much love. On a different note, she said, 'He hadn't stopped caring. He'll always care about High Valley.'

'I believe you,' said Kyle.

'The house needs a coat of paint.'

'It needs more than paint, Liane.'

'I'll get out my pad and make notes as we go.'

Kyle's hand tightened on hers, refusing to let it go. 'Mental notes will be adequate at this stage,' he said lightly.

They walked on, talking as they went. There were the things Kyle knew needed doing. There were also things that only Liane could have known: the spreading rot beneath the third step of the staircase; the banister that could do with some strengthening in one particular spot; the shutter that did not open completely, and the loose bricks in a hearth.

'I should let you deal with the contractors,' Kyle teased.

'Thanks, but no, thanks,' she said.

'I'm hoping you'll help me choose fabrics for new curtains and colours for the walls. New furniture too.'

'No, Kyle, my help is limited to today's suggestions.'

'I thought women loved planning the décor of a house.'

'They enjoy planning their own homes.'

'This was your home once, Liane.'

'It isn't any more.'

'It could have been again,' Kyle said, very softly.

Liane tensed. For a while she had been so absorbed in the house and all the necessary repairs that she had actually forgotten that he was still holding her hand. All at once she was conscious of every long, rough finger.

'It couldn't,' she said over a racing heart. 'We both know why you want to marry me. And besides, you've already made it clear that you never propose to the same woman more than once.'

'I did say that, didn't I?'

'Yes, you did.'

'Which leaves me—where?'

Was he talking about marriage or the house?

'With decisions that you'll have to make on your own,' Liane said firmly, deciding against giving him the satisfaction of asking him to elaborate on his question.

'My future wife might not approve of my choices,' he added.

If only the thought of another woman in Kyle's life did not hurt so much. Somehow Liane managed to say briskly, 'Either your wife will learn to live with your choices, or you may have to make a few changes.'

She found that she could not look at him as they walked further. She was in a hurry now, wanting only to get through the rest of the rooms as quickly as possible, so that she could leave High Valley and return to the cottage.

She declined to linger in the main bedroom which had once belonged to her parents. One day Kyle and his wife would probably sleep there. He asked her whether pink and grey would go together well in the room.

'Pink and grey are lovely,' she said, her voice low. 'But people's tastes are individual, and I'm not prepared to impose what I like on someone else. Especially not in the most personal room of the house.' With which she looked pointedly at her watch. 'It's getting very late; I really do have to go.'

'In a few minutes,' he said, then he led her into her old room.

'This would be very nice for guests,' Liane said.

Kyle laughed softly. 'Even nicer for a child, don't you think?'

She looked at him curiously. 'This isn't the first time you've mentioned children.'

'I'd like to be a father. Just think, Liane, if things had worked out differently, you and I might have had children together by now.'

The blood drained from her cheeks at the words.

'What's wrong?' he asked.

'Nothing.'

'You're very pale suddenly. Did I say something to upset you?'

'No!'

'We were talking about children. Is that it? The thought of a baby scares you?'

Here was her chance to tell him about the past. She opened her mouth, and the words, You and I conceived a baby together, trembled on her lips. In that moment she pictured Kyle's reaction. Already he felt such bitterness towards her grandfather; if he were to know that Grant Dubois had kept the fact of her pregnancy from him, his fury would know no limits. She could not cope with that kind of anger. Not now, not today. One day she would have to tell him, of course—he deserved to know that there had been a baby. But she had to prepare herself first. And so she swallowed down on the words.

'Don't you want children, Liane?' he asked.

'Eventually,' she managed to say.

'Well, then, what is it? What's wrong?'

'Nothing. Maybe I just had too much sun.'

'Nonsense. You're used to being out of doors; it can't be that.'

She had to distract him. Quickly.

'There's one repair you'll need to make in this room,' she said.

'Oh?'

She went to the window and opened it.

'There's a dent in the sill.' She turned to him, forcing a brightness she was far from feeling. 'Remember the night you climbed the wall to my window? The heel of your shoe left a mark in the wood.'

'Good heavens!' His eyes sparkled with the memory. 'I'd forgotten about that night.'

'I'd forgotten too. But I came to this room a few weeks ago. The day we met, in fact, the day I gave you the key. I was saying my farewells to the house, and I saw the mark.'

She was talking with animation, hoping to distract him from the topic of babies.

The ruse was working, for he was absorbed in memory now. 'The sill was higher than I realised, and I landed on the floor with a thud.'

'Right!' she smiled.

'How could I have forgotten? It was all I could think of that day—how I was going to go to your room that night.'

She had been able to think of nothing else either. The years vanished as she remembered lying fully dressed in the dark room, her window open, her ears attuned to every noise outside—the shrilling of the crickets, the croaking of a frog—and then, at last, the sounds she'd been waiting for—the whisper of careful footsteps, the soft creak of the creeper. She remembered the dread of being caught, a dread that had been superseded by the excitement of spending an illicit hour with Kyle.

He was laughing. 'It was the most daring escapade of my life until then. But in the end I was so terrified that your grandfather might have heard that thud—to my frightened ears it was as loud as a cannon shot—that I didn't stay more than a few minutes.'

'His room was near by. He could have walked in and surprised us.'

Kyle took a step towards her. 'He isn't in his room now, Liane.' There was a new note in his voice, and his eyes were on her lips.

Liane began to tremble.

He took two more steps, closing the distance between them. 'We have the house to ourselves.'

'I . . . I have to go.'

'There's nobody here to surprise us.'

'I told you—I have to go.'

'Not yet.' His voice was husky and seductive.

'Kyle . . .' She tried to move past him.

But he caught her in his hands, holding her shoulders. 'I remember how much I wanted you that night, but we were both nervous. There's nothing to keep us back now, Liane.'

He was so close to her, filling her nostrils with an indefinable masculine smell that she remembered of old. He looked down at her, and she saw the way his eyes moved over her body, lingering on her lips and her throat, going to her breasts and down to her hips. For no apparent reason her eyes filled with tears. His gaze moved upwards again, and when he saw the tears he made a noise in his throat. Then he was reaching for her, pulling her trembling body against him. He began to kiss her, and this time he did not have to coax her lips apart—they parted instinctively. His tongue traced the outline of her mouth before entering it, exploring the sweetness, letting his teeth nibble at the soft inner part of her lip.

There was familiarity in the feel of him, in the taste of him, but there was newness too. The young Kyle had not known how to kiss with such sensuousness. Deep within Liane a fire raged. She could not have stopped Kyle, even if she had wanted to. Half crazy with desire, she had no defences against him. Her arms were around him, drawing him closer against her, glorying in the hard feel of him as their bodies fitted together.

She could not have said afterwards how long they kissed. When he lifted his head and said, 'Liane,' she could only look at him mutely.

'Liane...' he said again.

She did not want to talk. She wanted him to kiss her again. There were so many empty years to make up for, so many lonely nights when she had dreamed of making love with him.

'Marry me,' he said.

For a second the words filled her with an indescribable pleasure. Still dizzy with the passion of his kisses, her only thought was to say yes. *Yes, my darling, yes!* And then her eyes cleared and she saw him looking down at her.

'Marry me,' he said again.

In a rush, memory came flooding back. And then she had her hands against his chest, and was pushing herself away from him.

'*Never!*' She gave a violent shake of her head.

'Anyone would think a proposal was an insult.' His voice was flat.

'From you, to me, it is.'

'A moment ago you were so passionate, Liane. I believe you'd have let me love you all the way, if I'd wanted to.'

What he said was true. Liane knew that if Kyle had wanted to take her to bed she would not have stopped him. Fortunately, that had not happened.

'You're an expert at seduction,' she threw at him.

'Are you really going to tell me you didn't enjoy what we were doing?' he taunted.

'You wouldn't believe me if I did.'

'Darn right I wouldn't. Mind telling me why you're so angry?'

'I don't like being manipulated.'

'And I was manipulating you, of course.'

'Why else were you kissing me?' she demanded. 'You aroused me—yes, I admit I was aroused. But then you're an expert. And it's all part of your plan. Excite me enough, and I'll agree to do anything you ask. You know so well how to do it. Did you have a few good teachers, Kyle, or did you acquire all your expertise naturally?'

'Careful, Liane.' His eyes were cold as steel. 'You're saying too much; you may have regrets later.'

'Not for a moment. I see through you, Kyle Avery. You want me to marry you so that you can complete your revenge against my grandfather. That's what the seduction scene was all about, wasn't it? Well, you can forget it! You have High Valley, but you'll never have me!'

Liane was huddled against the wall now, on the furthest side of the room from Kyle. She did not see that his eyes were particularly bleak.

'Don't ask me to marry you again,' she threw the words at him savagely, 'because my answer would only be the same every time.'

A muscle moved in his throat. 'Don't worry, I won't.'

Still trembling, Liane moved to the door. She did not look back as she left the room. And when she left the house she did not turn her head to see if Kyle was watching her.

When Liane arrived at the office on Monday, she was greeted with the news of an upcoming wine-sellers' convention. Her working days, always full, became even more frenziedly busy. As public relations officer of the winery, she had the responsibility of making sure that the company would be well represented at the convention.

Liane, who had recognised early that public relations was a career to which she was well suited, had always enjoyed the phone calls, the interviews, the meetings with the media. Now she welcomed the heightened activity for another reason: it kept her mind occupied.

Four days went by. Driving home from town every afternoon, she would see the familiar long fence of High Valley come into view, and she would fix her eyes firmly on the road ahead. She did not want to catch as much as a glimpse of the lovely gables. She did not want to meet a long silver car. High Valley—and its owner—had no more place in her life.

On Thursday she was home later than usual. Her grandfather was in the living-room, reading an agricultural magazine, when she arrived. Liane kissed his cheek, then put down her belongings.

As always, there was a cool drink waiting for her. She sipped it gratefully, leaning back in her chair and absorbing the restfulness of the room. It was a far cry from the spacious reception areas of High Valley, but in its own way it was lovely too. Liane and her grandfather had managed to save some cherished pieces: a Persian rug, a stinkwood kist, a few nice chairs, a mahogany table which had graced High Valley's living-room for more than two hundred years. On the table was an earthenware jar filled with proteas and dry grasses, and on the kist was a grouping of family photos.

'Any calls for me?' Liane asked when she had finished her drink.

'Two.'

'Oh?'

'Both from the same person. That man—Avery.'

'*Kyle* phoned?' Liane sat upright in her seat.

'Weren't you expecting to hear from him?'

'No.'

'Told you the man was trouble, and I was right,' grumbled her grandfather. 'You've been out of sorts ever since you spent the day with him.'

'Did he say what he wanted?'

'Asked you to phone him. The nerve of the man, and I almost told him so. Only restrained myself for your sake. Not going to return his calls, are you?'

'I might, but not before I've made us some supper.'

She put down her glass and went to the kitchen, but her mind was not on the meal she cooked. She had assumed she would not be hearing from Kyle again. And now he had phoned, and she did not know if she wanted to speak to him.

They had almost finished their meal when the phone rang.

'Thought I'd try you again,' came Kyle's voice. 'On the off-chance that you'll have dinner with me tomorrow evening, I've reserved a table at André's.'

André's was one of the most elegant restaurants in the town. Liane held the telephone tightly. 'Why?'

'Time for planning session number two.'

His cheerful tone took her by surprise. 'Are you saying the party's still on?'

'Of course. And I presume you're still my hostess.'

'I don't know what to say... I thought that after Saturday things would have changed.'

'I won't propose to you again—that's a promise. But the party continues as planned.' He paused a moment, then added, 'With or without you, Liane.'

She could picture the glint in his eyes. 'Kyle...'

'Everyone on the list has accepted. Except for Elsbeth Barber, and she'll be away a few weeks.'

'I see...' Liane felt a little dazed. 'When you set out to do something, you certainly do it quickly.'

Kyle laughed. 'I've told you about my guest list—how did you get on with yours? Is your grandfather coming?'

Liane glanced at the man in question. He was not even making a pretence at eating his meal, but was listening to her conversation with interest. 'I haven't invited him yet,' she said.

She didn't feel like telling Kyle how uncertain she had been of her own attendance at the party.

'Invite him, Liane. You can tell me his decision when we meet.'

'But I'm still not sure whether——'

'We'll talk tomorrow. See you around eight.'

There was a soft click as Kyle put down his phone. Liane looked at her receiver a moment, before putting it down with more force than was necessary. She glanced once more at her grandfather, and saw that his eyes were alight with curiosity.

At André's the next evening, Kyle declined to talk about anything concerning the party until they had finished their meal. They spoke about themselves instead. Liane was already acquainted with the main events of Kyle's life since he'd left High Valley, but there was so much more she wanted to know. He was a good conversationalist, making her laugh with frequent anecdotes, able to turn a joke against himself. He wanted to know about her as well. She told him about the degree she had taken in Cape Town, and about her stint on a daily newspaper, all of which had led up to her present position at the winery.

'I feel as if I'm getting to know you all over again,' Kyle said at length.

'I feel the same way,' Liane agreed.

'The lovely young girl has turned into a beautiful woman who's made something of herself.'

She smiled at him. 'I certainly don't think anyone could have predicted the direction *you* would take.'

'That's true. Isn't this *good*, Liane, sitting together, talking, just enjoying each other's company? We haven't argued even once tonight.'

She looked at him across the table. There was a candle between them, and the flickering flame cast a shadow across his face, softening the customary hardness of his lips and jaw, turning his eyes into deep, dark pools. Kyle would have been a wonderful father, firm perhaps, yet loving.

She swallowed on the tears that blocked her throat. 'It's very nice,' she said unsteadily.

'Liane?' He was watching her intently. 'What's wrong?'

'It's nothing, really.'

'You're obviously upset.'

'It's not something I want to talk about.'

'On Saturday, at High Valley, you were upset too.'

'Not really.'

'The sun had nothing to do with it, we both know that. What's wrong, Liane? Don't you feel able to confide in me?'

'Not about this. Leave it, Kyle, please... It's been such a lovely evening, don't let's spoil it.'

Their food came just then. The meal was excellent: stuffed trout in a delicious wine-flavoured mushroom sauce, tender asparagus, and tiny buttered potatoes. Dessert was a wonderful strawberry soufflé. And this time Liane was not surprised when Kyle ordered a good wine.

It was only when the last plates had been taken from the table that he said, 'Shall we get down to business?'

Liane brought out her pad and pen, and they began to discuss party fare. When they had their menu planned,

Kyle said, he would call in a catering service to prepare it.

Emotions under control once more, Liane was able to smile easily again. 'Doesn't it seem sacrilegious to talk about food after the incredible meal we've just eaten?'

He smiled back at her. 'A little ironic, perhaps.'

'Not that anything you and I might dream up could possibly compete, of course.'

'André would be glad to hear you say that—I gather he doesn't like competition. But we can let our imaginations run wild anyway.'

Liane had searched some of her recipe books for ideas, and Kyle listened with obvious interest while she talked. Half an hour went by and a party menu began to take shape—half an hour in which they laughed and teased and debated, and realised that while they had some culinary tastes in common they did not share the same views on exotic foods like snails and caviare.

'About the flowers,' Liane said, when the menu was complete.

'I don't think so,' said Kyle.

'You don't want flowers at your party?'

'We'll discuss flowers another evening.'

Liane glanced at her watch. 'We have time now. It's not that late.'

'I like to deal with one topic at a time.' He grinned at her. 'We'll talk about flowers next time we meet, wine the time after that. And then, of course, we'll have to go out for dinner so that we can arrange the music.'

Liane was conscious of something quickening inside her as she looked through the candle-light into the face of the most attractive man she had ever known.

She danced him a smile. 'Why do I get the feeling that you're really a bit of a rogue?'

His eyes sparkled back at her. 'Haven't a clue. By the way, you still haven't told me whether your grandfather is coming to the party.'

'I haven't asked him yet.'

'I think you should,' he told her.

They rose to go soon after that. Kyle held Liane's hand as they left the restaurant and walked to the car. They didn't talk much on the drive back home. Kyle turned on the radio and they listened to guitar music. Liane put her head back against the seat, closed her eyes and drank in the sweet-smelling air that came through the open window.

He walked with her to the cottage. At the door, he cupped her face in his hands and kissed her lightly on her lips.

'Friday?' he said.

'Yes.'

'We'll talk about the flowers then.'

'All right.'

'Goodnight, Liane.'

'Goodnight, Kyle.'

She was smiling as she watched him vanish in the darkness.

On Friday, Kyle took Liane to a restaurant where they danced as well as dined. The next week they went out together twice, once to a trendy little diner, once to a cottage in the mountains where the atmosphere was so romantic that Liane found herself wishing they could kiss instead of talk.

'I'm certain the party will be a success,' Kyle said, when all their plans were made at last.

Liane was certain of only one thing: seven years ago she had fallen in love with Kyle Avery—she knew now that as long as she lived she would never love anyone else.

CHAPTER FIVE

'How do I look?'

Eyes that had watched over almost every phase of
Liane's life swept her now. Grant Dubois' gaze took in
the new silk dress, deep jade in colour, moulding softly
to Liane's figure, just snug enough to suggest the
roundness of hips and the curve of her breasts, and the
antique pendant and matching earrings which had belonged to her mother. But his gaze rested longest on her
face—on lips tilted in a smile, flushed cheeks and eyes
that sparkled with excitement.

'You look very beautiful,' he said gruffly, and she saw
a look of pain pass over his face. 'I remember the first
time your father brought your mother to High Valley.
They were so much in love, couldn't wait to be married.
She was radiant, and so full of life. You remind me of
the way she looked then.'

Liane was moved. 'Thank you.'

'I only wish you *didn't* have that look, *liefie*. I wish
Kyle Avery had never bought our property. I wish we
didn't have to have anything to do with the man. I wish
to God he'd never come back into our lives—*your* life,
in particular.'

'But he did buy High Valley. And now I know that
I'll always——' She stopped herself, and said, 'Change
your mind and come with me, Gramps.'

The old man shook his head.

'Kyle invited you,' she persisted.

'He won't miss me for a second. No, *liefie*, I don't like the man, I don't trust him, and I refuse to go to his party.'

Liane glanced at her watch. 'I promised Kyle I'd be there early, before any of the other guests arrive.'

'Liane...' Her grandfather was beside her, his hand on her arm, his eyes unusually concerned. 'Be careful.'

She smiled at him. 'It's customary to tell a person about to go out for the evening to have a good time.'

'I want you to be careful of him, *liefie*.'

'All right, if it'll make you happy. Goodnight, Gramps, and don't wait up for me.' She hugged him, and walked out of the cottage.

Within minutes she was at High Valley. Stopping the car on the brick pad, she sat quite still for a few seconds, looking up at the house. She had been here most of the day, overseeing the last-minute preparations—the platters of food, the positioning of the flowers, the low platform where the musicians would sit. Chaos had reigned for a while, but by the time she had left to go home and get dressed there had been order.

How lovely the house was tonight, she thought, with lights shining in every window, and the high gable a graceful curving line against the cloudless sky. On each side of the door stood a tall clay pot filled with cascading flowers, red and blue and yellow. The pots had been Liane's idea. 'Let's even have flowers outside the house,' she had said to Kyle, and he had welcomed the suggestion.

He must have heard her arrive, for as she left the car she saw the door of the house open, and there was Kyle, walking down the steps towards her.

The breath stopped in her throat as she looked at him. Though the invitation had mentioned formal attire, for some reason she had not pictured Kyle in a tuxedo with a ruffled shirt and a black bow-tie. The elegant clothes could so easily have robbed him of some of his normal toughness; instead the tough air was heightened. He looked even taller than usual, lithe and tanned and athletic. Dangerously seductive.

'Liane.' He took both her hands in his, and she saw something move in his face as he looked down at her. After a long moment he said, 'You look very beautiful.'

It was an echo of her grandfather's words, but the look Kyle gave her was altogether different. It was a thoroughly male look, appreciative, assessing, piercing the simply cut jade dress to the body beneath it, making no effort to hide his thoughts.

Suddenly the blood was surging through Liane's veins. Her grandfather's warning forgotten, she smiled up at Kyle with sparkling eyes.

'Am I the first one here?'

'You are—as befits the hostess.'

Hostess... When he had first broached the idea, she had tried to resist it. With the realisation that she was in love with Kyle, that she had never stopped loving him, the word had a wonderful sound.

'Your grandfather didn't come after all,' he said.

'No, I'm sorry.'

'Couldn't bring himself to consort with the enemy?'

'He... he isn't one for parties any more.'

'You don't have to make excuses for him, Liane. I understand perfectly. I didn't think Grant Dubois would come.'

She looked at him anxiously. 'Don't be hurt, Kyle.'

'Hurt?' His eyes were hooded suddenly, impossible to read. 'I doubt if your grandfather still has the capacity to hurt me.'

Desperate to sustain the mood of a few moments earlier, Liane said brightly, 'The evening's going to be fun. We used to have such wonderful parties here.'

'I know—I told you how I peeped in through the windows. Of course, the stable-boy was never invited.'

They were at the door now, and she stopped and looked up at him. 'You don't miss an opportunity to point out the differences between us, do you?'

'Are you trying to say they don't exist?'

She hated the hardness in his face and the challenge in his tone. 'Perhaps they did...then...but they don't any longer. You're a successful man now, Kyle. People look up to you. There's nothing you can't do, can't have.'

'Except you.'

The words didn't have the sound of a proposal. There was nothing in them to justify the leaping of her heart. True, he had asked her to marry him twice, but if he was serious about his intentions he would have to say that he loved her. Anything else could never be enough. And she sensed that she would never hear those words from him.

'People will be arriving soon. I want to take a last look around,' she said, and walked past him into the house.

An hour later, looking exultantly around her, Liane saw that all her expectations for the party had been fulfilled. The house throbbed with the sound of talking and laughter and music. In the dining-room a buffet supper graced a long table; there were platters of chicken and duck, salads and speciality breads. On another smaller table were the desserts—cakes and trifles and a big dish of exotic fruit. The guests ate and drank and gathered in groups, enjoying the company of people they knew well but did not meet often.

Kyle was everywhere, moving easily from one room to another, talking to this group and to that, teasing the women, flirting with them, exchanging a joke with the men. Liane saw how they all warmed to him. The men

recognised the appearance of a powerful new presence
in their community; the women were dazzled by his
rugged good looks and his sensuous manner. There
would be women who would dream of Kyle Avery tonight, Liane thought.

Not once did Liane, moving among the guests too,
hear a derogatory reference to Kyle's former position at
High Valley. There were many who seemed to know he'd
worked here once—he was quite open about the fact—
but to see Kyle Avery, vital and elegant in his tuxedo,
was to forget that his situation had ever been humble.

When dinner was over, the dancing began. The three-
piece band Liane had suggested to Kyle was known for
its liveliness, and in no time many of the guests had taken
to the dance-floor. Liane was claimed almost right away
by Ted Lawrence. Ted, a man in his late thirties with a
mop of unruly red hair and a moustache that he had
never been able to tame into any semblance of tidiness,
no matter how hard he tried, was the son of one of Grant
Dubois' lifelong friends. He had always been fond of
Liane, treating her as a much younger sister. She had
been just entering her teens and about to go to her first
dance when he had taught her a few rudimentary steps.

'You do me credit,' he laughed, when they had gone
twice around the dance-floor together. 'Light as a feather
on your feet, and so easy to lead.'

She grinned up at him. 'Says wonders for your
teaching abilities!'

'To have learned anything from a dancer as rotten as
I am, you must have been a natural.' He held her a little
away from him so that he could look down into her face.
'I heard your grandfather was upset when he found out
it was Kyle who'd bought High Valley.'

Liane hesitated a moment. 'He wasn't happy,' she admitted then, 'but I think he's accepted it.'

'It'll be interesting to see what Kyle does with the place. I don't recognise the fellow at all. Quite impressive, isn't he?'

After Ted, Liane danced with others. Some had been contemporaries of her parents, a few were much younger; many had lived in the valley for as long as Liane. Not all the guests were farmers, however. There were people from town as well, people Kyle had put on the guest list himself, builders and industrialists, engineers and a well-known banker. Each one spoke in approving terms about High Valley's new owner.

'May I have this dance?'

One melody had just ended, another was beginning. Liane turned at the sound of the familiar voice, then smiled up at the man with whom she had been dancing. 'I've enjoyed this, Michael, but I think our host wants to have a turn with me.'

'I've been waiting for this,' Kyle said as he took her into his arms.

She slanted him a laughing look. 'If that's true, you certainly took your time about asking me.'

'Only because I wanted to get all my obligations out of the way first. I don't think there's a woman I missed out.'

'Noble of you.'

'I thought so,' he agreed with a smile, and drew her closer.

As if Kyle had given the band a signal, the music changed, becoming softer and slower than it had been all evening. Liane, who had also been waiting for her dance with him, leaned her head against his chest and closed her eyes. As they moved slowly around the floor, she revelled in the feel of him; his shirt was crisp against her cheek, but beneath it she felt the hardness of his chest and the strong pounding of his heart. His hands were on her back, sliding sensuously over the soft silk dress, and his thighs moved against hers in a rhythm that was so erotic that she did not know how she could contain her excitement.

She could not have said how long they danced together. Only when the music stopped, and Kyle loosened his arms, did she open her eyes. The band had been playing without pause for over two hours; it was time for the musicians to have a break.

Kyle kept one arm around her shoulders as they walked over to the bar. A few other guests, thirsty from dancing, were there too. Kyle got Liane and himself each a glass of wine.

'Hey, Kyle, what are your plans for the vineyards?' The questioner was Bill Harris. Bill had recently taken over his father's wine estate. He and his wife, Sandy, had been schoolfriends of Liane's.

'I don't intend making any radical changes there,' Kyle said. 'The vineyards look healthy, and I mean to keep them that way.'

'Will this be your permanent home?' Sandy cast a quick glance at Liane as she posed the question.

Liane held her breath, waiting for the answer.

'I have business interests in other parts of the country, but yes, I hope to be here most of the time.'

'Glad to hear it.' Ian Taylor had entered the conversation. He was an old-timer, a man who had worked his land almost as long as Grant Dubois. 'I don't believe in absentee farmers.'

'I agree with you,' Kyle said.

'Say, Kyle . . .' Bill again ' . . . do you have any ideas for the fields on the east boundary? Nothing's been done with them in years. I suppose you'll be putting down vineyards there too?'

The east boundary was a few yards from the cottage where Liane and her grandfather lived. Just the other day, walking across the empty fields, Liane had wondered what Kyle would do with them.

'Actually,' Kyle said, 'I've been thinking about building a little shopping centre.'

It took a few moments for the words to make an impact on Liane. When they did, she went rigid.

There were gasps of surprise from the people standing around them, and Bill whistled. 'A *shopping* centre! Are you serious?'

'Perfectly.'

On the pretext that she had finished her drink and was still thirsty, Liane took a step away from Kyle. The waiter filled her glass almost to the top; her hand shook so badly that the liquid was in danger of spilling. Looking up, she saw Ted's eyes on her face, his expression one of concern.

In minutes a crowd had formed around Kyle, most of the party guests drawn to him by his unexpected announcement. Questions flowed, one after another.

'A shopping centre?'

'How big?'

'Can you build shops on farmland?'

'When will you start?'

'Have the plans been approved?'

'Whoa!' Kyle held up a hand, and Liane saw that he was smiling. 'I'll tell you as much as I can.'

He was able to get that portion of the land re-zoned for business purposes, he said. He had made all the necessary enquiries, and there would be no problem with building shops on those particular fields. No, he did not envisage anything on a big scale.

'Shopping centre's too grand a term for what I have in mind really. It'll be a farmers' mall,' he explained. 'At the moment many of you have to drive into town to do your shopping. What I have in mind is a small supermarket. There'll be a shop for farming implements, for cattle feed and riding equipment, things like that. I was even thinking of a restaurant.'

A restaurant... People dining till late at night within earshot of the cottage. Raucous music, cars hooting, the squealing of brakes. Liane felt sick just thinking about it. Her grandfather would hate it with a vengeance!

'What about access from the main road?' Sandy Harris had always been practical.

'No problem there either,' Kyle told her. 'Apparently it'll be easy enough to lay a road alongside the property fence.'

'You've thought it all out,' Ted Lawrence said slowly.

'I've made it my business to do that.' Liane caught the crispness in Kyle's tone, the decisiveness and the daring which had enabled him to transform himself into a successful entrepreneur.

More questions. Hearing Kyle's announcement, Liane had been certain his guests would be dismayed and shocked by the very thought of commercial development in what had always been farmland. She saw that she was wrong. Apart from Ted Lawrence's, every face revealed interest. For the townspeople—the builders, the engineers and the banker—there was the prospect of money and jobs. As for the farmers, none of them would be affected by the mall. Not one had property anywhere near the east boundary. If anything, everyone seemed excited by Kyle's proposal. It would mean an end to the long drive into town whenever they needed food or farming supplies. And a restaurant, in an area where there was little entertainment, was particularly welcome.

Would any of them spare a thought for Grant Dubois? A few, but not many, Liane suspected. He'd always been a difficult sort of man; most of them would say that if he was upset by the idea of a little mall that was too bad, wasn't it? He would have to get used to the development beyond the fence. If he couldn't accept it, he could always live elsewhere.

Liane felt more ill by the second. A throbbing had started at her temples, increasing to the point where she felt as if her head would explode from the pain.

Ted was looking her way once more, and she moved her eyes in the direction of the library, indicating by gesture that she wanted to speak to him.

In the library, Liane sank down in a chair and pressed her hands to her aching head. 'Can he do it, Ted?'

'Sounds like it, doesn't it?' The eyes of the man she had known and trusted all her life were troubled.

'How can he use farmland for a mall? It isn't possible.'

'You heard him, Liane. Kyle Avery's no fool. If he says he's gone into the question of re-zoning, he must know what he's talking about.'

'He has to be stopped,' she insisted.

'Perhaps he can't be.'

'I don't accept that,' she said grimly. 'I simply don't accept it. I have to find a way of stopping him, and I will. I don't know what it will take, but whatever it is I'll have to do it.

'We have to talk,' Liane said, when the last of the guests had gone.

'I'd like that.' There was a smile in Kyle's eyes. 'I thought the party went well, didn't you?'

'From your point of view, I suppose it did,' she agreed.

'Meaning?'

'You set out to charm those people, and you succeeded. The rich and handsome host in his elegant tuxedo. You waved your wand and enchanted the lot of them. They've accepted you, Kyle, just as you wanted. They'll do more than accept you—they'll beat down your door with invitations. You'll be the most eligible bachelor for miles around. So yes, the party was a success—a huge, rip-roaring success.'

'As the hostess that should please you,' he pointed out. 'And yet you're as angry as I've ever seen you.'

'You don't need me to tell you why.'

'You will anyway, I've no doubt.'

Earlier, Liane had requested a pain-killer from a woman who was known to carry an assortment of medicines in her handbag, and by now, to her relief, the worst of her headache was gone. She was able to talk to Kyle without hammers of pain striking at her temples.

'The farmers' mall!' she flung at him.

'So that's it.'

'Don't pretend to be surprised—I couldn't take that.'

'I realised you were taken aback by the news.'

'"Taken aback"? That's putting it mildly, Kyle. I'm still reeling.'

'I'm sorry.'

He made to take her hand, but she stepped quickly out of his reach. Just a few hours ago she had been in his arms on the dance-floor, her eyes closed, her mind on the moment when the last guest would have departed High Valley, leaving her alone with him. They would make love then, she had thought. She would summon the courage to tell him how she felt about him. She might even tell him about the baby.

Looking at him now, dangerous as a panther in his black tuxedo, it was hard to believe that such a short time later everything could have changed.

'You're not sorry about a damn thing! If anything, you enjoyed the shock value of your announcement.' She threw the words at him. 'Do you know, before I left home tonight my grandfather warned me to be careful of you?'

Dark eyes glinted in the rugged face. 'I've done nothing to harm you,' Kyle said evenly.

'You're about to. Why did you never tell me about your plans, Kyle? You could have so easily.'

'Maybe I didn't feel I owed you any explanations, Liane.'

'Rubbish! You insisted that I be your hostess. You were so keen that your wretched party should go well. Obviously you thought that if I knew your plans for the land I wouldn't co-operate.'

Kyle did not answer. There was something ominous about his silence, but Liane was far too angry to be frightened of him.

'This is just one more part of your revenge,' she stormed.

'Is that how you see it?'

'How else can I possibly see it? Those fields have always been farmland. Other than revenge, there's no reason to have them re-zoned.'

'Every reason,' he said, quite reasonably, as if he actually expected her to listen to him, to believe him. 'Nothing has been done with those fields for years. And why? Because the earth in that spot isn't as good as it should be. Like it or not, Liane, I don't work in the stables any more. I'm a businessman now, with a businessman's way of looking at things. I don't believe in holding an unproductive asset, and that's what the fields on the east boundary happen to be.'

It was Liane's turn to be silent. There was a small grain of truth in what Kyle was saying, she admitted to herself. Apart from the eastern portion, most of the High Valley land was fertile. Her grandfather had made an attempt to farm the fields in question, but without success. Generations of his predecessors had had no luck with them either. Kyle, who had lived at High Valley until he was twenty-three, would have known why the fields had never been cultivated.

'Perhaps that particular land isn't the most fertile, but maybe you could find *something* that would grow there,' she said slowly.

'I doubt it. Anyway, I prefer my idea.'

'I *hate* it!'

'You're making too much of it, Liane. The development won't bring glitz and noise and crowds. It will be exactly what I said—a little farmers' mall. A place where people from around here can buy what they need without going all the way to town.'

'It will be a monstrosity.'

'You're wrong. I have in mind something rural and artistic. Something that will blend with the countryside.'

Everything Kyle was saying made sense. Except for one thing.

'You can't do this to my grandfather.' Liane's voice was very low now.

'Really?' A dangerous light had appeared in Kyle's eyes. 'Do you mind telling me why not?'

'He looks across those fields every day of his life. He sits on the *stoep* and he looks across the land to the mountains. He loves High Valley, Kyle. Selling it hasn't changed his feelings for the place. He still thinks of it as his home, even now, when it no longer belongs to him. This . . . this mall of yours . . . it would destroy him.'

'*Destroy him*? Do you think your grandfather ever questioned what he was doing to my father?'

Liane heard the passion in Kyle's tone and saw the sudden pallor in his face. She tried to shrink from him as he advanced on her, but she did not move quickly enough. An iron hand gripped her wrist.

'That was some speech you just made, Liane—obviously meant to elicit my sympathy. You might even have succeeded—except for one thing. I've never forgotten what Grant Dubois did to us. Do you think he spent one sleepless night afterwards, wondering how my father felt when he was kicked off the property with just one hour's notice? Did *you* think about it? If you did, you haven't mentioned it.'

'Kyle...'

'Your grandfather destroyed my father just as surely as if he'd put a gun to his head. Dad was born at High Valley, did you know that? Like me, he started off in the stables. He was always so proud of what he did. He used to tell me about the horses he'd cared for, about the Dubois children he'd taught to ride. Later, when he progressed to other work on the farm, he taught me to take pride in my own work. You say your grandfather thinks of High Valley as his home, even now, when he no longer owns it. Well, to my father this place was home too. He was born here, he lived here, he thought he'd die here. In the space of minutes he lost that home. No home, no work, nowhere to go. Dad had no idea what you and I had been up to in the barn. He was in total shock when we were evicted.'

'I'm so sorry,' Liane whispered inadequately.

'There's more,' Kyle continued. 'A few months after we left High Valley, Dad died.'

'*No*!'

'Yes. He wasn't an old man. I believed then, I still believe now, that he died of a broken heart.'

Liane was shivering now, but Kyle seemed not to notice her distress. His hand still gripped her wrist, painfully, relentlessly.

'God, Kyle, I'm so sorry,' she whispered.

'Sorry!' he said derisively. 'Is that the best you can come up with?'

'I know it's not much, but I don't know what else to say.'

He glared down at her. Beneath dark winged brows his eyes were wild and stormy.

'Sorry!' he said again. 'Maybe you really are sorry about what happened—*now*—but at the time you did nothing to prevent it.'

'There's nothing I could have done.'

'You could have come to us. Helped us.'

'No...' Tears choked her throat, but she swallowed hard to keep them down. This furious, bitter Kyle would not be swayed by tears. If anything, they would enrage him further.

'You could have followed your grandfather,' he threw at her.

'No...' she said again.

'You could have reasoned with him. You could have told him the truth. You could have told him that I never forced you to do anything you didn't want to do. Maybe it wouldn't have changed anything, but at least you could have tried. Instead you remained quietly out of sight in the safety of the house. You stayed silent. I suppose you couldn't bring yourself to tell your grandfather that you wanted sex as much as I did. You were the princess, the adored one. Nothing was allowed to change that.'

His savagery was unnerving. Liane battled for composure. She had to calm him somehow. One day he would have to know the truth about their baby, but this was not the right time. The telling could only be done quietly, calmly, with as little emotion as possible.

'There are things you don't know,' she whispered unsteadily.

'There are things you don't know either, Liane. Things I haven't told you until now. Did you know that your grandfather beat me?'

She was horrified. '*No!*'

'Yes.'

Kyle dropped her hand. Without warning he threw off the elegant tuxedo jacket, yanked the ends of his white shirt out of his trousers, and lifted the shirt up towards his shoulders.

He turned his back on Liane. 'There!'

She shrank back. Without quite understanding why, she knew she did not want to see whatever it was he was trying to show her.

But Kyle was unmoved by her reluctance. '*Look*!' It was a command.

'I don't want... I can't...'

'You can! You've been shielded too long. It's time you saw. Time you knew.'

'Kyle, please...'

'Look, Liane! Damn you, woman, look!'

She did look then. Nausea leaped in her throat as she saw three scars on Kyle's back. Even after so long they were still there, faded now, faint, but still visible.

This time there was no suppressing the tears that filled her eyes. 'I wish I'd known. Oh, Kyle, I wish I'd known.'

'What would you have done?'

She stepped closer to him. Tentatively she reached out a hand, moving it towards his back, hovering just inches above the faded scars.

'What would you have done?' There was a new note in his tone, as if he knew that he had shocked her; as if, in some part of him, he even felt some small bit of compassion for her.

'I'd have tried to comfort you.'

The hand that hovered above Kyle's back descended, very slowly, until it was touching the scars. Kyle flinched. In a second his body was rigid.

Liane's voice was shaking. 'I'd have done everything I could to comfort you. I wish there was something I could do now.'

'It's too late for that.'

'It's not too late to tell you I'm sorry.'

'For my father it's too late,' he said harshly.

Recognising that there was nothing she could say, Liane remained silent. The scars on Kyle's back were like magnets, holding her eyes, forbidding them to move away. How *could* you, Gramps? she thought. She ran her fingers over the scars, and then, almost without thinking, leaned forward and touched them with her lips.

Kyle made an agonised sound in his throat. In one swift movement he turned, lifted her into his arms and carried her out of the room and down the passageway.

'Put me down,' she ordered. 'Put me down!'

He did not respond. He just went on walking, quickly, as if she weighed nothing at all, through the door of the house, letting it slam shut behind him. He strode out into the darkness of the night, with Liane pounding on his back with her hands and demanding to know where he was taking her.

When he turned on to the path that led to the barn, she knew where they were going. Excitement flared inside her. All day she'd wanted to make love with him, but the scene she had envisaged was a gentle one, with the two of them kissing for a while after all the guests had left and before she went back to the cottage. This headlong dash into the night was something else again. Mixed with a mounting desire was a sensation of intense fear.

In the dark the path seemed even more desolate and overgrown than in the daytime. Leafy twigs caught Liane's hair, and once a branch tore at her dress. The night insects filled the air with their shrilling, and somewhere quite near by something, a mouse perhaps, skittered over some loose stones.

Kyle strode on, undeterred by any branches or stones in his way, by tiny unseen animals in the undergrowth. He was like a man possessed.

They reached the barn and he shoved the door aside with his foot. He put Liane down, abruptly, so that for a moment she swayed on her feet. There was a moon that night, and with the door of the barn ajar there was just enough light to distinguish shapes. She could not see Kyle's face clearly, but she was able to make out the shape of him, could sense the urgency of his stance, could hear the unsteadiness of his breath, and knew he was staring at her just as she was staring at him.

Suddenly he was reaching for her. She went to him willingly. So great was her desire that when he pulled her into his arms her arms went around him too.

In seconds they were kissing—passionate kisses, searching and hungry. Kyle's hands began an exploration, shaping themselves to Liane's throat, her waist, her hips. His shirt was still loose, and she reached for his scars, touching them, caressing them, tracing a path along them as if she needed to know their exact shape and size.

She did not resist when he pulled down her zip in one quick, abrupt movement. He tugged the dress from her shoulders, and as it fell to her feet she stepped out of it without thinking. Just as quickly he unclasped her bra, and when that was gone his hands were on her breasts, his fingers playing with nipples that hardened at his touch, his lips kissing where his fingers had been. Liane's hands were as eager as his, unbuttoning his shirt, sliding her hands over his chest, his shoulders, re-learning the shape of his body, a body that had grown hard and muscled with the years. Her eyes were closed now. All her actions were born of desire, of instinct, of love for this man whom she had never stopped loving.

When he lifted her into his arms and put her down on the ground she did nothing to stop him. The ground was rough against her skin, but she did not care. If anything, the roughness heightened the eroticism of the moment. She wanted Kyle to love her.

Only this time she would make sure she was protected. Years ago, a few minutes of thoughtless pleasure had created unhappiness that would never be forgotten or erased. She could not let the same thing happen again. Man of the world that Kyle was now, he would have something with him, but she would have to make certain.

She was about to ask the question when he said harshly, 'This was a mistake.'

She looked at him through dazed eyes.

'A mistake,' he repeated, pushing himself away from her.

'Kyle...' she whispered, reaching for him.

But he resisted her. 'Blame it on me—I got carried away. We have to stop this, Liane.'

'If you didn't want this, you shouldn't have started it.' She was quivering with humiliation.

'Do you think I don't know that? My God, Liane, your fingers on my scars, your lips... You don't know what you did to me! I went mad. All I could think of was making love to you.'

'Is there something wrong with that?'

'Damn right there is! I don't matter to you. I never have. The only person you've ever cared about is your grandfather. I should have understood that a long time ago; I was a fool that I didn't. It's not important to you that he behaved like some feudal tyrant. All that matters is that his peace of mind shouldn't be destroyed.'

Liane was a bundle of frustration, aching for the fulfilment only Kyle could give her. But his furious words had to be answered.

Sitting up, she held her dress against her breasts. 'I'm not blind to my grandfather's faults,' she said painfully. 'I feel terrible about what he did—*shocked*! But I can't just stop loving him. He's all I have, Kyle.'

'That's why this is wrong for us.' The simple words had a hopeless sound. 'I may have changed, Liane, but you never will. Before anything else, you'll always be Grant Dubois' granddaughter.'

Liane sat up. She was trembling. 'I'd better go home.'

'Yes.'

They both dressed in silence, a silence that endured as they left the barn and walked back along the dark path. Liane remembered that her bag and her car keys were still in the house; Kyle waited outside as she went inside to fetch them.

She was opening the door of her car when he spoke again. 'I don't want to see you again, Liane; there's only turmoil every time we meet.'

She flinched at the unfairness of his words. 'Nobody asked you to buy High Valley.'

'Perhaps it was a mistake. The fact is, I did buy it, and it's my home now. Thanks for being my hostess tonight, but stay away from me from now on. I'm human and I have normal desires. I'll only end up regretting it if I make love to you, and I don't know how much self-control I have left.'

She was glad it was too dark for him to see the tears that stung her eyes. 'Goodnight,' she said as she got into the car.

By the time she turned the key in the ignition, Kyle had vanished in the darkness.

CHAPTER SIX

LIANE jerked upright in bed, screams coming from her throat and her body wet with sweat. It was a few seconds before she understood that she'd been having a nightmare—a particularly vivid one. Kyle had been in it, her grandfather too. Gramps had been advancing on Kyle, stick in hand, and she had been trying to stop him.

Shuddering, she lay back against the pillows. A nightmare... In the days after the miscarriage and after Kyle had left High Valley there had been many nightmares. Those nightmares had been worse, far worse, than the one from which she had just emerged. But this one had been bad too.

It was strange that her cries had not brought her grandfather into the room. And then she saw the sun streaming through the windows, and she knew it had to be mid-morning. Gramps would be outside. It was not often that she slept so late.

Her limbs ached as she got slowly out of bed. On the chair by the window she saw the jade dress. She had not hung it in her wardrobe last night, but had thrown it on the chair instead, as if, with the party over, she had no more use for it. Picking it up, she ran her fingers over the dress. The feel of the silk brought back the feel of scars beneath her fingers.

Abruptly she crumpled the dress into a tight ball and pushed it behind her shoes at the back of her wardrobe. She would never wear it again, she was sure of that.

For a long time she stood under the shower. When she was dry she pulled on jeans and a T-shirt and ran a comb through her wet hair. She did not bother with make-up. She went to the kitchen, opened the fridge, then decided she wasn't hungry. All she wanted was a cup of strong coffee. When that was made she took her cup, and one for her grandfather, and went outside.

Grant Dubois was sitting in his usual wicker chair on the *stoep*. The sleeping dog lay at his feet, the Sunday papers were open on his lap, but he was not reading. As usual he was smoking his pipe, and his eyes were on the peaceful land beyond the fence. He had not noticed Liane.

How frail he looked, as if a wind could push him over. Three years ago there had been the bad fall from the ladder. He had injured his back and legs, and his mobility had been permanently impaired. A year later there had been the near-fatal bout of pneumonia. For weeks Liane had feared for his life. Grant Dubois had recovered, but the man who had once had such power in his body was only a shadow of his former self now. Looking at him, she found it hard to believe that just seven years ago he would have had the strength to beat Kyle. But there it was; Liane had seen the scars, and she did not doubt the truth of Kyle's words.

'I brought you some coffee,' she said quietly.

Ash dropped on his sweater as he turned his head. 'Why, *liefie*, good morning.'

'Morning, Gramps.'

Liane put down his cup on a small round table by his side, and sat down as well. She took a few sips of her coffee, then closed her eyes and let the sun warm her face.

'You slept late today,' observed her grandfather after a while.

'I was tired,' Liane said without opening her eyes.

'Didn't hear you come home.'

'I came in quietly. I didn't want you to wake.'

'What time was it?' he asked.

'After two.'

'Good party, Liane?'

'OK.'

'That's it? After all the work you put in for that man, that's all you have to say—OK?'

'People seemed to enjoy themselves,' she said.

'Talkative this morning, aren't you?'

'Don't push it, Gramps, please.'

'Just being sociable. I expected you up hours ago, singing the praises of Kyle Avery's great house-warming party.'

'I'm not in the mood to be baited about Kyle this morning, Gramps.'

'I don't mean to bait you, I'm just curious. Are you all right, Liane?'

She opened her eyes, and found him watching her shrewdly. 'Why do you ask?'

'I just think you're looking a bit peaky. Not your usual self at all.'

'Put it down to the late night,' she told him.

But Grant Dubois was not to be side-tracked. 'You say "people" enjoyed themselves. Did *you* enjoy yourself, Liane?'

Liane hesitated. Kyle's disclosures had given her a new perspective on her grandfather, so that when she had returned to the cottage last night she had thought things could never be the same between them again. Briefly, she had even toyed with the idea of leaving him and finding a flat for herself in town. Yet looking at him now, seeing the man her grandfather had become, knowing that there were only the two of them in the world and that they had to stand together, she was inclined to give him the easy answer—it was a wonderful party, she'd had a great time.

But there were things she had to know.

She put down her cup. 'We have to talk, Gramps.'

'About?' His eyes had narrowed.

'Kyle.'

'We've talked about nothing but Kyle Avery for weeks.'

'I need to know what happened that night. The night you forced him out of High Valley.'

A variety of emotions came and went in Grant Dubois' face: anger, pain, even some fear. 'It happened so long ago,' he said then.

'There are things that don't vanish with time, Gramps.'

'What are you trying to tell me?'

'Kyle still has scars.'

He seemed to flinch. 'Scars...?'

'For years I thought he left High Valley right after my fall... *before* I actually miscarried. I thought he couldn't deal with my pregnancy. Then you told me you'd asked him to go, but you never said how. I was sure you'd given him an ultimatum, that he went because you threatened him in some way.'

'Liane...'

'That wasn't the way it was, was it?'

'I struck him,' Grant Dubois said grimly.

At the thought of the scars she had seen the previous night Liane felt sick. 'It was more than that, Gramps. It must have been quite a thrashing.'

'Kyle's been complaining to you, has he?' he growled.

'Until last night, he'd never told me what happened. Even then I might not have believed him—but I saw the scars on his back.'

'You saw scars... How, Liane? *Why*? Dear God, this is what I've feared ever since he came here. I told you to be careful of the man. I knew he was trouble. Is it all going to start again, Liane? What were you doing with Kyle Avery that you would see him without clothes?' Grant Dubois' voice rang with angry passion.

'I'm twenty-four years old, Gramps.' Liane was angry too. 'I'm a woman now, and what I was doing with Kyle is my concern. The fact is that I saw him without his clothes on. I saw the scars. I want to know how they got there—and why.'

'Liane... *Liefie*...' The old man's gaze left her face and went to his beloved fields. When he spoke again, the fierceness had left his voice. 'Perhaps what I did was wrong. Perhaps I went too far with Kyle; I see that now. But you have to understand how it was. When your parents died I was wild with grief—my only son, and the beautiful young woman I'd come to regard as a daughter, both gone. But I had to come to terms with the loss. You were there, and I had to go on living. There we were, a crusty widower and a little girl. I was the only person you had, and I had to make a life for you. Can you even begin to imagine how I felt? What did I know about little girls, Liane? I'd never had a daughter, and my wife brought up our son. But I was determined to do all I could for you. I gave you all the love that was in me.'

He paused. Liane saw him dab at his eyes, and was swept with compassion. Whatever her grandfather had done, it was in the past now. She put her hand over his, the gnarled veins touching at her heart.

'It's all right, Gramps. Don't go on...'

He turned back to her. 'I have to. This... this can of worms is open now, and it won't be closed until we get things clear between us.'

'I think I understand,' she said gently.

'I have to make sure you do. I watched you grow, *liefie*, and I knew that there were things I couldn't do for you, couldn't tell you. You needed a mother, yet I was all you had. You grew into your teens. You became more and more lovely, and I was terrified. I realised that the boys would soon be after you, and I didn't know how to warn you, how to prepare you. I just kept hoping you'd be all right.'

'And then Kyle came along,' Liane said softly.

'He didn't come along exactly, he'd always lived on the farm. But he was so much older than you, and somehow it never occurred to me that he'd be attracted to you. I should have guessed, I suppose. Even when I realised how much time you were spending together I wasn't worried. I thought—*stupidly*—that Kyle was grooming your horse, improving your riding skills, that kind of thing.'

'And then you found out I was pregnant.'

'I'll never forget that night, sitting in the waiting-room of the hospital, waiting for the doctor to tell me if you'd suffered concussion. And then the horror—the absolute horror—of hearing the man tell me that my grand-daughter was expecting a baby. I knew the father had to be Kyle; it couldn't be anyone else. And in fact you admitted as much. When I got over the shock, I was wild with anger, Liane. I wanted to kill him; that's how furious I was. I sped back to the farm and went out looking for him. I didn't mean to hit him, you have to believe that, but anger gave me a strength I didn't know I still had, and I...I suppose I just lost control. Kyle was so confused that he didn't even try to fight back. Afterwards, I told him to get out. I told his father to leave too.'

Liane listened to the story, her feelings a mixture of understanding, disgust and sadness—understanding at why her grandfather had behaved with such violence, disgust at his loss of control and the pain he had inflicted, sadness for herself, and for Kyle, and for all they had lost.

'And now you've met Kyle Avery again——' Grant Dubois' voice was low and unhappy '—and you can't forgive your grandfather for what he did.'

Liane left her chair and, still holding her grandfather's hand, she knelt at his side. 'You did a terrible thing, Gramps. I can't say otherwise because I'd be making light of what happened, and I can't do that. Did you know that Kyle's father died a few months after they left the farm?'

'Yes, and I was very upset about it. Jim Avery was a good man.'

'Kyle thinks he was unable to live anywhere else but at High Valley.'

'I can't undo what I did, *liefie*.' There was a great sadness in the old man's voice.

'That's true, you can't. I'm glad we've talked, Gramps, even though it hasn't been easy for either of us. I had to hear these things from your lips as well as from Kyle's.'

'Can you forgive me, Liane?'

'I wish none of it had happened, but you're my grandfather—how can I not forgive you?'

'Do you mean that?' Hope flickered in the faded eyes.

'I know that you did what you did because you loved me.'

'That's the way it was,' Grant Dubois said huskily. 'I don't know what else I can say except that I'm sorry. I couldn't let Kyle remain at High Valley, but I wish I hadn't hurt him. More than that, I wish I hadn't hurt his father.'

And now Kyle was about to hurt her grandfather in a way he could not anticipate.

They were silent a while, Liane and her grandfather, absorbed in their thoughts.

It was Grant Dubois who broke the silence. 'I'm the weak one now, Kyle is the strong man. I don't know how many years I have left to me, but there are things I'm thankful for. I have you, and although I no longer have High Valley at least I live close enough to the farm to make believe it's still my home.'

'Gramps——' Liane began, knowing that her grandfather had to be warned about the coming development on the other side of the east boundary.

'Do you know,' he went on, as if he had not noticed the interruption, 'I spend hours looking out over the land? When you're at work I spend most of the day out here. I look across the fence, over it, as if it didn't exist. I'll never forgive myself for making that stupid investment and losing your inheritance, but as long as we're in this cottage, as long as I can see the land that used to belong to my family, I can let myself believe we're still connected to it.'

'Oh, Gramps,' Liane said in a strangled voice.

'Can he do it, Ted?'

'He can, Liane.'

Liane had gone to Ted Lawrence when she'd tried to reach Martin Simpson, the lawyer, and been told he was out of town. Ted's expression was serious.

'There must be something we can do to stop him,' she said.

'I wish there was, but I've gone into the matter quite thoroughly. I went so far as to phone my own lawyer, and he did some checking for me. It's a little complicated to explain, I'm not sure I understand it completely myself, but Kyle Avery can have those fields re-zoned. He has to meet certain provisions, of course, but he can do that quite easily. The man isn't a fool, Liane—I told you that the night of the party. He'd obviously been into all the legalities himself a long time ago.'

'Then you're saying there's absolutely nothing we can do?'

'Short of going to court to fight an expensive case you'll probably lose—no, I don't think there's anything you can do.'

A few days later Martin Simpson, back from his trip, gave Liane the same advice. Kyle was free to build his farmers' mall.

'What does your grandfather think of the plan?' Martin asked.

'He doesn't know about it,' she told him.

The lawyer leaned forward, his fingers interlaced on top of his fine mahogany desk.

'You're surely not intending to hide this from him, Liane?'

'That's exactly what I intend doing—until I'm quite sure there's no way out.'

'There's nothing to stop Kyle Avery building that mall.'

'I don't believe that,' Liane said grimly.

Preparations for the wine-sellers' convention were well under way by this time. Liane's desk was covered with papers of all kinds—pamphlets and schedules and pictures. The tape on her dictaphone was filled with letters and Press releases and memos. It seemed as if the phone never stopped ringing, and the fax machine was in constant use.

The vice-president of the winery invited her to a business lunch. She was a natural public relations woman, he told her. He was impressed with the speakers she had managed to line up for the convention, and the publicity it was being given in the Press. A substantial salary raise was in the offing.

Normally Liane would have been thrilled with all the praise she was receiving. Yet by the time she left the office and began to drive home the luncheon talk had left her mind. Now she could concentrate on only one thing—how to stop Kyle from going ahead with his plans.

She had never felt quite so confused. On the one hand, she could not blame Kyle for not caring if Grant Dubois was hurt by the farmers' mall that was to be built virtually on his doorstep. On the other hand, the thought of what the mall would do to her grandfather tore at her heart.

The fact that she loved both men did not make it easier for her.

After a week of fruitless tossing and turning, the idea came to her quite suddenly in the early hours of a Sunday morning. Excitement jerked her upright in bed. Looking at the clock, she saw that it was only just after three. Somehow she would have to wait until daylight.

'Going somewhere?' asked her grandfather a few hours later, when she came on to the *stoep*, her bag slung over her shoulder, her car keys in her hands.

'I have to see someone,' she told him.

'Who?'

'A friend.'

'When will you be back?' As if he sensed her excitement, he was eyeing her with interest.

'I don't know. It depends on—our discussion. There's a stew in the fridge, Gramps. Warm it up if I'm not here in time for lunch.'

She could have walked across the fields, but she took the car because she did not want to arouse her grandfather's curiosity. Her fingers were trembling, so that it took her half a minute to fit the key in the lock.

It didn't take long to drive the short distance to High Valley. Liane was relieved to see the silver car on the brick pad. Kyle was here, and she would talk to him before she lost her courage. She took a deep breath, then got out of the car, walked up the steps, and knocked on the thick wooden door. As she waited for Kyle, she felt the hard beat of her pulse in her throat.

And then there he was.

'This is an unexpected visit,' he drawled.

'You . . . you said you never wanted to see me again.'

'I remember.'

'I don't know if you meant it...'

'I did at the time. Put it down to frustration. We were both over-emotional that night.'

'Then you don't mind my coming?' She tried to smile; she did not want him to sense her nervousness.

'No, though I admit I'm surprised to see you.'

'Yes, well...' Her throat was growing drier by the minute. 'I have to talk to you. Can...can I come in?'

'Of course.'

She followed him to the library. This had always been one of Liane's favourite rooms. Though much of the original furniture of the house had been sold, the mahogany floor-to-ceiling bookcases, built by a master craftsman and attached to the walls, remained. Kyle's books lined the shelves now; if Liane's plan was successful she would have time to read them. If not... But the plan had to succeed.

'I don't remember—did I ever tell you I like the way you've furnished this room?' she asked jerkily.

'You did. Thanks anyway.'

'The curtains are just right, that particular shade of gold... And the Persian rug is gorgeous—wherever did you find it?'

'I bought it from a dealer in Cape Town; we talked about that too.' Kyle's voice was dry. 'This isn't the first time you've seen the library, Liane, and I don't believe you're here to comment on my choice of furnishings.'

'No...'

'I've never seen you so nervous. Why don't you sit down and tell me what this is all about?'

If she was nervous, he was the picture of confidence. A wicked sparkle warmed his eyes and his lips were tilted at the corners. His hair was slightly damp, as if he'd just been for a swim; dark and glossy, it curled a bit against his neck, and for one insane moment Liane longed to bury her hands in it.

'Well, Liane?' His amusement deepened. 'It's not like you to be at a loss for words. Are you going to tell me why you're here?'

'I want to marry you.' The words tumbled quickly from her lips.

'Good *heavens*!'

'You're surprised...'

'That's some understatement.'

'Will you, Kyle?'

'Not without knowing a hell of a lot more about this unexpected proposal.'

Her fingers played nervously in her lap. 'It was your proposal to begin with.'

'I remember. I also remember that you turned it down. Firmly. And more than once.'

'Yes. But now I'd like to accept.' Nervousness was making her throat so dry that it hurt to speak. 'Why are you looking at me like that, Kyle?'

'I'm wondering why you've changed your mind. Are you going to tell me you've fallen madly in love with me?'

'Of course not...' she began, and stopped.

A little muscle moved beneath Kyle's jaw.

'So that's not it,' he said evenly. 'I didn't really flatter myself that it was.'

Liane's neck and face were moist with perspiration. She could not remember when she had felt quite so awkward. In the darkness of her room, her idea had seemed so simple. For the first time she understood how foolish she'd been not to realise that Kyle was too perceptive a person to take her proposal at face value.

'You wanted to marry me a few weeks ago.' Her voice shook.

'Correct.'

'Why don't you want to marry me any more now?'

'Do I have to remind you again that you turned me down? You've also admitted you're not in love with me. So now I'm asking you—why are you suddenly so eager to be my wife?'

'Does . . . does there have to be a reason?'

'Damn right there does,' Kyle said flatly. His eyes were cold. 'You're after something, Liane. What is it?'

'I don't think there's any point in going on with this,' she said painfully. 'You've already given me your answer.'

'Actually, I haven't given you any answer at all.' Their chairs were quite close together, and his hand shot out and grabbed her wrist. 'What are you after, Liane? I need to know.'

She was silent.

'Talk!' he ordered.

'My grandfather . . .' she said unsteadily.

'Ah.' Kyle did not look at all surprised.

'Your mall . . . It . . . it will destroy him, Kyle.'

'And you think if I married you I'd be prepared to forgo my plans?'

'I hoped you would.'

His fingers were like the rest of him—hard as steel. Liane forced herself to look at his face, and saw that his expression was hard too. Evidently she had under-estimated him. Once Kyle's feelings for her had been as strong as hers were for him—or so she had believed. But with time they had changed. Her simple idea had been just that—simple.

'I guess I've been naïve,' she whispered.

'You're right there,' he agreed.

She pulled her hand out of his and stood up, turning her head away from him, hoping he would not see the tears in her eyes.

She was at the door when his voice stopped her. 'Where are you going?'

'Home.'

'Do you always give up so easily when you want something?'

She lifted her chin. Defeated she might be, but she still had her pride. 'What is there for me to stick around for?'

'Sit down. We haven't finished our discussion.'

Something in his voice caught her, so that she looked at him. 'We haven't?'

'Let's just say I'm interested. If I were to accept your proposal—*if*, Liane—what would there be in it for me?'

'I thought that was obvious.'

'I want to hear you spell it out.'

He was so self-assured, so confident. Liane knew she could tell Kyle nothing that would surprise him. If he insisted on hearing her put her idea into words, it was only because he enjoyed torturing her.

'All along you've wanted to revenge yourself on my grandfather,' she said slowly. 'That's why you bought High Valley. You told me yourself it was only one part of your plan.'

'Go on.'

'When you asked me to marry you, it was because that way you could complete your revenge.'

'You have it all worked out, don't you?' he observed drily.

'You never left me in any doubt, Kyle. You've been after revenge all the time. If you married me, you'd have what you always wanted. There'd be no more need for you to go ahead with a mall which might not even turn out to be very profitable. I mean, there's no way of telling how well it would really do.'

'True,' he admitted.

Feeling helpless and vulnerable, Liane shifted her feet. All she wanted now was to get away from him. Never mind that she loved him, at this moment she felt she never wanted to see him again. But the ball was in her court once more. He was waiting for her to speak.

'I thought... It seemed to me that if we got married there'd be something in it for both of us.'

The dark eyes held hers, his gaze so enigmatic that it was impossible to guess what he was thinking.

'You may be right,' he said after a long moment.

She took an unsteady breath. 'Does that mean you're agreeing to my proposal?'

He kept her waiting for what seemed like eternity. Except for the slight upturn at the corners of his lips, his face was without expression.

And then, quite pleasantly, he said, 'Yes.'

Liane stared at the man she'd fallen in love with seven years earlier, whom she loved even more deeply now. By rights, this moment should be one of sheer bliss. Instead, she felt utterly miserable.

'There is only one thing——' she began, only to stop at the sound of the phone.

Kyle left the library. The telephone was in the entrance hall, and Liane could hear his voice, though she could not make out the words. The call had come at the wrong time, interrupting her as she was about to tell him that the marriage could only be one of form. They would never live together as man and wife.

She turned her head as she heard the click of the receiver and he came back into the room.

'Kyle...'

'Something's come up,' he said, 'a weekend office emergency. I'm sorry, but I have to draw up an urgent document right away.'

'But Kyle——'

'I have to fax it within the hour. We'll talk again another time, Liane.'

Unhappily, with a sense of things being unfinished, she stood up. She could see he was in a hurry, but there

was something she had to ask him all the same before
she left.

'I have to know, Kyle... Are we engaged?'

'Of course.' He gave her a dry look.

And then he bent his head and kissed her lightly on
the lips. It was the emotionless kiss of a person who was
sealing a bargain. Love had not the slightest part in it.

All the rest of the day Liane was in turmoil. Now and
then she saw her grandfather looking at her, his eyes
curious, his expression disturbed. It was obvious that he
knew something had happened, but until she spoke to
Kyle again, and made certain he'd meant what he'd said
about marrying her, she could not tell her grandfather
that she was engaged.

In the late afternoon, they sat together on the *stoep*.
The sun was almost down. The distant mountains were
an indistinguishable mass against the sky, and the valley
was cloaked in the dimness that settled on the land just
before night. Only the fields beyond the fence still held
some small remnant of light.

Looking at the fields, wondering if they were now safe
from builders and bulldozers, from crowds and cars and
shoppers and noise, Liane did not hear the car that drove
along the sandy road and stopped beside the cottage.

'I think Kyle's here,' said her grandfather.

Moments later Kyle appeared on the *stoep*.

Liane rose unsteadily to her feet. She had half expected he might come, and had rehearsed what she would
say to him. Yet now that he was here she was searching
for words.

As it was, Kyle spoke first. 'Well, have you told your
grandfather our news?'

'What news?' demanded Grant Dubois quickly, before
Liane could say anything.

'Gramps——'

'*What* news?'

'So you don't know, Mr Dubois? Evidently Liane was waiting for me, so that we could tell you together. That was very considerate of her.'

'If you have something to say, Mr Avery, just plain say it,' snapped the old man.

Kyle drew Liane to him and put his arm around her shoulders. 'Your granddaughter and I are engaged to be married.'

A visible shudder ran through the old man, so that for a moment he looked even frailer than usual. Then he seemed to draw upon some hidden reserve of strength.

'Is this true?' He did not look at Kyle; his eyes were only on Liane.

'Yes.'

Pulling away from Kyle's arm, Liane took a step towards her grandfather. She was about to say something more, but Grant Dubois had already risen to his feet. Head erect, ignoring her obvious distress, he left the *stoep* and walked into the house.

'Did you have to do that?' Liane demanded when the door of the cottage was closed.

Kyle gave an unrepentant shrug. 'May I remind you that you proposed to me this morning?'

'I don't need reminding—the humiliation is still vivid. But you didn't have to spring it on him like that, Kyle!'

'He had to know.'

'I would have told him in my own time.'

'Would you have mentioned our deal?' he asked.

'No.'

'He must have heard about my plans for those fields.'

'He hadn't. We live such a quiet life here. So few people come by, there's nobody who'd have told him.'

'And you hadn't said anything?' queried Kyle.

'I thought I'd wait...until...'

'Until you knew if your little scheme would work?'

'I only thought of it during the night.' Liane lifted her head. 'My grandfather's reaction to your news must have pleased you, Kyle. At least you can't be in any doubt about the success of your revenge.'

Kyle did not answer. It was so dark now that Liane was unable to read his expression.

'There is one thing,' she said after a few moments. 'I was going to talk to you about it this morning, but then the phone rang and you had all that work to do.'

'Well?'

'I'm sure it's obvious.'

'If you have something to say, say it.'

'Our marriage can only be in name, Kyle.'

'Meaning?'

'We won't live together as man and wife.'

'No sex?'

'Right.'

'Let me get this quite straight. You come to my house and propose marriage to me, and then you set your own limits to the bargain?'

She bit her lip. 'I was sure you'd understand.'

'You're hardly a virgin bride.' The words were hard and derisive.

Liane's throat was tight. 'People have to love each other to make love.'

Kyle laughed. The sound was rough and raw in the darkness. 'Since when is that a fact?'

'It has to be that way with me,' she insisted.

Liane was certain Kyle would argue the point. Surprisingly, after a small silence, his next words concerned a different topic altogether.

'When do you want to be married?'

She was taken aback. 'As soon as you like.'

'You'll need time to prepare.'

'I won't need much time if we have a simple wedding,' she assured him.

'It won't be simple. On the contrary, I want to see you in a long white dress, with a veil covering your face and a huge bouquet of roses in your hands. A reception on the lawn of High Valley.'

'None of that is necessary,' protested Liane.

'It is to me.'

'All these trappings—are they part of your revenge?' she asked slowly.

'It's the way our wedding will be,' said her fiancé in a take-it-or-leave-it tone. 'I'll pick you up after work tomorrow and we'll go and choose a ring.'

'You mean a wedding-band.'

'You'll have that too. Tomorrow we'll buy a diamond.'

CHAPTER SEVEN

'IS THIS really what you want?'

Liane was standing at the kitchen table, preparing dinner. She had made a vegetable soup the day before, and now she was slicing a loaf of crusty bread while the soup simmered in a pot on the stove.

Without turning, she said, 'Would I have got engaged otherwise? Why do you ask, Gramps?'

'You and Kyle Avery—it's quite a shock.'

'You must have known it could happen,' she said.

'I've been dreading it from the moment that man came back into our lives,' Grant told her.

'I wish you wouldn't talk like this,' Liane said unhappily. 'That man, as you insist on calling him, is going to be my husband. You're all the family I have, Gramps. I want you to accept him; it's very important to me.'

'I'll try. For your sake I really will try. But I have to tell you, there's something about this whole affair that makes me uneasy.' Grant Dubois sounded troubled.

'That's nonsense.' Liane attempted a laugh that didn't quite make it. She wondered if her grandfather could have registered the sound as a sob.

'Are you happy, Liane?'

'Good grief, Gramps, what kind of question is that to ask a girl who's about to be married?'

'I remember the night your parents announced their engagement. Their happiness was so intense, you felt you could touch it. You don't have that look, *liefie*.'

'On the night of Kyle's party you were grumbling that I looked radiant,' she reminded him.

'I remember, but you haven't been yourself at all since then. If anything, I'd have said you were miserable.'

Liane could not keep her head averted any longer without confirming her grandfather's suspicions. It was time to put the meal on the table. As she ladled the soup into bright earthenware dishes, she forced herself to smile.

'Do you think that maybe you're imagining things, Gramps?'

'Maybe I am,' said her grandfather as they sat down together. 'Tell me one thing, Liane—do you love him?'

'With all my heart.' That answer, at least, was simple.

'I can't possibly accept this.'

Liane looked in dismay at the ring which Kyle had insisted on placing on her finger.

'Don't you like it?' He sounded amused.

'It's exquisite.'

'Then there's no problem.'

She looked at Kyle and back at the ring. It was the most beautiful piece of jewellery she had ever seen—an enormous pear-shaped diamond surrounded by tiny emeralds. She felt like a princess with that ring on her hand.

'It's far too expensive,' she murmured.

'Don't think about the expense, Liane.'

'I can't take it, Kyle.'

'If you like it, and you obviously do, I want you to have it.'

Liane shot a quick glance at the salesperson, an experienced auburn-haired woman, smartly dressed and beautifully groomed, who seemed to have sensed that Kyle was in the market for quality, and that money was of no concern to him. The rings she had taken from a locked glass cabinet were all expensive. When Liane had inspected one velvet-lined tray, the woman brought out a second tray, and then a third. If she was aware that Liane was embarrassed by the price tags, she did not show it. A few minutes earlier the manager had approached her with a question, and she had moved aside to answer it. For a few seconds Liane and Kyle could talk without being overheard.

Softly Liane said, 'I'd have been happy with just a simple gold band, but if I must have an engagement ring let's take something smaller.'

'No.'

'This isn't right for me, Kyle.'

'It looks wonderful on your finger.'

At that moment the salesperson returned to them. 'Is there something else I can show you?' she asked.

'Thank you, but I think we've made our decision,' Kyle said. 'My fiancée and I like the ring she has on now.' He smiled at Liane. 'Don't we, darling?'

Liane could only nod as she took the ring from her finger and handed it over to be boxed.

Fiancée... Darling... How easily Kyle used the words—darling in particular. That word would never be said other than in public, and only to reinforce their charade. He would never know how she longed to hear the endearment on his lips when they were alone together, and spoken with love.

Suddenly tears welled in Liane's eyes. Kyle was paying for the ring now, and she walked to the other side of the shop, where she pretended to study a showcase of bracelets while she tried to regain her composure. By the time Kyle—her *fiancé*—came up beside her and said, 'Anything else you fancy, darling?' she was able to shake her head with a smile.

He took her hand as they left the shop. His car was parked outside.

'Dinner,' he said, as he opened the door for her.

'Don't tell me we're going out for dinner now?'

'Of course.'

'I thought you were going to take me home.'

'I will—after we've celebrated our engagement.'

'Our deal, you mean.' The words were out before she could stop them.

One eyebrow lifted. 'If that's what you prefer to call it.'

'We both know it's a deal, and I hardly think it's something to celebrate.' She looked at him squarely. 'Unless, of course, you need to savour your revenge.'

'Savour—I like that word.' Kyle gave her an unrepentant grin. 'It will be more fun if we savour it together.'

Liane was not surprised when he stopped the car outside the restaurant where they had eaten the first time. Nor was she surprised that they were given the best table once more. Or that a bottle of chilled French champagne was brought to them even before the meal had been served.

When the champagne had been poured and they were alone, Kyle took the small velvet box from his pocket. Dark eyes holding hers, he opened the box and took out the ring.

'Give me your hand,' he said softly.

'In private, Kyle. Not here...'

'Give it to me.'

Liane was trembling as she lifted her left hand from her lap and placed it on the table. She loved Kyle so much. In the years since they had been parted she had never loved anyone else. There would never be another man for her. Their engagement should be tender and beautiful, and she wanted to weep at the fact that it was a charade instead.

Kyle's eyes were still on hers as he took her hand. He held it quite gently for a few seconds before slipping the ring on to the fourth finger. For a long moment Liane's hand lay motionless on the white tablecloth. She stared, as if mesmerised, at the lovely diamond which seemed to sparkle with a life of its own. Then she pulled her hand back abruptly and clenched it beneath the tablecloth.

Kyle laughed. 'You'll get used to wearing it.'

'I'm not so sure about that.'

'We don't have to argue the point.' Lifting his glass, he motioned to her to lift hers. Reaching across the table, clinking her glass with his, he said, 'To us, darling.'

His gaze was on her face as he took a sip of his champagne. Without thinking, Liane sipped from her glass too.

'Let's be happy together,' he said softly, continuing the toast.

'You like to taunt me, don't you?' She looked at him angrily.

'Is that what I'm doing?'

'What else is it when you call me darling and insist on buying me the most beautiful ring in the shop?'

'I'd say it was fairly common behaviour for a man who's just become engaged.'

'Not when he can't stand the woman he's engaged to. Oh, you're an excellent actor, Kyle, I have to give you that. Nobody seeing us clink glasses or watching you put the ring on my finger could possibly guess that you were just playing a role.'

'Am I?'

'You know you are. It's a mockery to pretend we're happy when we both know that we're not.'

'We could be,' he said quietly.

Her head jerked at the words. She looked at him, but his expression was enigmatic, his eyes impossible to read.

'It would be nice,' she said uncertainly.

'It's not impossible, Liane.'

For one wonderful moment she let herself hope. Perhaps Kyle really did believe they could be happy together. And then Liane remembered the circumstances of their engagement, and a momentary light died in her eyes.

'We both know why we're going into this marriage,' she said dully. 'You want revenge, and I'm letting you have it. This marriage of ours is nothing but a sham, Kyle. That's why I feel so awkward wearing this ring.' She lifted her hand and looked at the diamond. 'It's not as if I'll wear it forever.'

'Contemplating divorce even before we've reached the altar?' There was a strange edge to his voice.

'I'm just being realistic.' Her hand was back in her lap once more, and her eyes were unhappy. 'We never put a time-frame to the marriage——'

'Are you bringing up something new?' he asked.

'Not exactly. We've never discussed it, but it's obvious ours won't be one of those till-death-us-do-part unions. I guess we'll stay together until you feel your revenge is complete.'

'When will that be?' asked Kyle.

'That will be for you to say, won't it?'

'Definitely.' He laughed suddenly, his eyes sparkling at her across the table. 'Another toast, Liane.'

'Haven't you heard a thing I said?'

'Every word. And I still want to make another toast to my beautiful fiancée—I can call you that, can't I? However long we remain together, Liane, let's make the best of the time.'

Kyle had put into words Liane's most ardent wish. Silently she picked up her glass and drank to his toast.

Liane was smiling to herself as she made her way through the fields early the next Saturday. She and Kyle were going to spend the day hanging up pictures and deciding on new curtains for some of the bedrooms. Several days had passed since their engagement, and despite the circumstances of their coming together Liane was beginning to feel very excited at the thought of going back to live at High Valley as Kyle's wife. Even her grandfather seemed to have accepted the wedding as fact, and had stopped referring to Kyle as 'that man'.

The door of the house was open, and she walked in. Kyle must have heard her, for he called, 'Just follow your nose, Liane.'

The smell of strong coffee permeated the house. Liane was laughing as she made her way to the kitchen, where she found Kyle, mug in hand, sitting at the table, the previous day's newspaper open in front of him.

'Pour yourself some,' he invited. 'It's freshly ground and brewed. Do you like strong coffee?'

'The stronger the better.'

'Funny how much there is we don't know about each other,' he remarked.

'There were things we didn't talk about seven years ago.'

'We'll have all the time in the world to talk about them now,' he said cheerfully.

If only that were true, Liane thought, but did not say so. Today was for hanging pictures, not for arguments.

When she had poured herself coffee, she joined Kyle at the table. The coffee was even stronger than she'd expected, and she sipped it slowly, savouring the good smell and flavour of the rich Brazilian brew.

Looking up, all at once, she saw that Kyle was watching her. 'What are you thinking about?' she asked.

He grinned. 'You.'

'Me?'

'Is that so strange? We're engaged, after all.'

'Kyle——'

'I was looking at you,' he went on, as if he had not heard the protest, 'and thinking how pretty you are. Your cheeks are rosy from your walk, and your hair must have blown in the wind, and I was just imagining what it will be like to sit across the breakfast table from you day after day once we're married.'

The words, with the images they evoked, created a tempest of longing. Looking at Kyle, laughing, virile, more handsome than any man had a right to be, Liane could easily visualise sharing her life with him. But only a life based on mutual love; anything else had to be meaningless.

She was glad when he said, 'Time to start hanging the pictures.'

She took his mug and her own, rinsed them both under the tap, then followed him out of the kitchen.

She had not known that Kyle was an avid collector of modern art—one more thing she was learning about him. When she had looked with great interest at all his pictures, they discussed where they should be hung. For two hours they worked together, Kyle holding a picture against a wall, Liane looking at it, telling him whether to raise or lower it, whether to move it to this side or that. And all the while they talked and laughed and joked, and the distance created by the years apart seemed to fall away, so that it was almost as if the violent separation had never occurred, and all the angry words of recent weeks had never been spoken.

They had just stopped for a second cup of coffee when the doorbell rang.

Liane looked at Kyle. 'Expecting someone?'

'Not that I know of. Do you think your grandfather's come to visit?'

'Unlikely,' Liane said, and Kyle went to the door.

A minute later he was back. With him was a young woman, reed-thin, dark-haired, beautiful.

'Elsbeth Barber!' exclaimed Liane in surprise. 'I thought you were away.'

'I was, but I arrived back yesterday and heard the news of your engagement.' Elsbeth kissed Liane on the cheek, then reached up to Kyle and kissed him too—on the lips, Liane noticed.

'This is so exciting,' Elsbeth said.

'Isn't it?' Liane responded lightly.

'Will you have some coffee, Elsbeth?' Kyle asked. 'Liane and I have been hanging pictures all morning, and we just stopped for a break.'

'I'd love some coffee.' Elsbeth's voice was low and more husky than Liane remembered it. She looked around her. 'This kitchen brings back so many memories. You and I were such good friends when we were at school, weren't we, Liane? I used to be here so often. Do you remember, Kyle?'

He grinned at her. 'I remember a long-legged kid who used to hang around the stables.'

'Those were good times, weren't they? That's why, when I heard about your engagement, I knew I had to come right over. Liane Dubois and Kyle Avery—what could be more perfect?'

A brilliant smile lit Elsbeth's face as she looked from one to the other. Liane watched her uneasily. There was something about Elsbeth's animation which she did not trust.

'It's wonderful, absolutely wonderful, that you two are going to be married. Fate must have brought you together again.'

'Fate?' Kyle said, with a dry look at Liane.

'Oh, yes, absolutely! I believe in fate, don't you? The two of you living here at High Valley where your romance began all those years ago—it's like a fairy-tale, isn't it?'

Kyle looked at Liane. There was no answer from either of them, but Elsbeth did not seem to notice their silence.

'I do hope you'll have a baby soon,' she went on.
'Only this time——'

Liane tensed. 'I'm dying to hear about your trip,
Elsbeth,' she interjected.

But Elsbeth was not to be diverted. 'I know things
will work out well for you this time.' The brilliant smile
was still firmly in place. 'I mean, for one thing, the two
of you will be married, and you won't be under such
stress, Liane. You'll be able to take good care of yourself.
No more silly accidents, no losing another baby.'

'I beg your pardon?' Kyle demanded.

Liane, giving him a desperate look, saw that he was
stunned.

'Well, it was so sad the way things turned out, wasn't
it? Liane miscarrying your baby, and all that. I'm quite
sure it won't happen again this time.'

Elsbeth looked at her watch and put down her cup.
If she was aware of the silence that had descended with
her words—and how could she not be aware of it?—she
did not show it.

'Heavens! That can't be the time!' she exclaimed. 'I
have an appointment and I'm late. I just dropped in to
congratulate you both, and to tell you how thrilled I am
with the news.' She kissed Liane's icy cheek and gave
Kyle's hand a squeeze. 'Please don't think I'm rude,
leaving like this before my cup is cold. You don't have
to see me to my car, Kyle, I can manage perfectly well
on my own. Well, all right, if you insist . . . Bye, Liane;
let's get together for lunch some time really soon. We
have so much catching up to do.'

Through the open window Liane heard the car drive
away. The blood seemed to have drained from her body,
and her legs felt so weak that she was barely able to
stand. She sank into the nearest chair.

She looked up as Kyle—a white-faced Kyle—strode
into the room.

'Well?' he demanded.

'Kyle...'

'Was she telling the truth?'

'Elsbeth was always a trouble-maker. I remember——'

'*Was she telling the truth*?'

'Yes,' Liane whispered. She shivered as she looked up at the man with whom, just a short while ago, she'd been joking and laughing and discussing the best place to hang his pictures. Kyle stood a few inches from her chair. In his ashen face his eyes were wild.

'You and I had a baby together, Liane?'

'Not exactly.'

'"Not exactly"? What's that supposed to mean? Either we had a baby or we didn't.' He had never looked so intimidating. 'Either I'm a father or I'm not.'

Liane gripped the sides of her chair. 'Kyle...'

'Talk!' he commanded.

'You're frightening me, Kyle. Sit down...please?'

'Don't tell me what to do. Talk, Liane.'

'I will, but it's really difficult when you tower above me like this. Please, Kyle, won't you sit?'

He stood above her, glaring at her, so that for a few seconds she wondered if he would heed her plea. Then, abruptly, he threw himself into a chair.

'Now,' he said ominously, 'talk. And don't leave anything out.'

Quietly Liane said, 'It's true—I was pregnant.'

'Seven years ago?'

'Yes.'

'With my child?'

She nodded. Her throat hurt, making it difficult to speak.

'Conceived on one of those nights when we made love in the barn?'

Once more she nodded.

'What happened to it? Where is it? Don't you understand, Liane, I have to know?'

'I do understand.'

Tears filled her eyes, but she dashed them away with her fingers. She did not want to cry. Kylc was an angry man, and she knew that tears would not sway him; if anything, they would only make him more furious.

Painfully, she said, 'I had an accident. A fall... I slipped on some oil in the kitchen. I was taken to hospital and...a few days later I miscarried. I lost the baby.'

'I have trouble taking this in.' His eyes were dazed with shock. 'I had no idea you were pregnant. Why didn't I know? I'd have married you if I'd known.'

'There'd have been no point,' she said with some difficulty. 'Not once I'd lost the baby.'

'Perhaps you wouldn't have lost it. Perhaps you wouldn't have fallen. The circumstances would have been different. You'd have been with me, not in the kitchen of your grandfather's house.'

'It's too late to speculate,' she said.

'Maybe. But why didn't you tell me, Liane? You saw me day aftcr day, we met in the barn all the time. Why did you keep your pregnancy a secret from me?'

'By the time I knew about it you were gone.' She swallowed hard on new tears.

'Go on.'

'I had no idea I was pregnant. I was only seventeen, Kyle, and I suppose I was very innocent. It seems hard to believe now, but that's the way it was. There were signs, but I didn't make anything of them. It never occurred to me that I might be having a baby. It was only when I was in hospital...after the fall...that I learned I was pregnant.'

Kyle's jaw was tight. 'I think I'm beginning to understand.'

'I was stunned, flabbergasted. I couldn't quite take it in, but my grandfather——'

'Was mad as all hell,' Kyle said crisply.

'Yes...'

'And so he rushed back to High Valley, beat me and threw me out of the place. My father after me.'

'He shouldn't have done that,' she said quietly.

'Damn right he shouldn't have. He could have told me what had happened. Could have asked me my side of the story. Could have found out how I felt before he picked up his stick.'

'He was wrong.'

'Without talking to me, he made up his mind that I'd seduced his precious granddaughter, his innocent girl who would never willingly have had sex.'

'I said he was wrong,' Liane said despairingly. 'He acknowledges that now. I know you won't believe this, but he really is sorry.'

'And you, Liane, why didn't you stop him? You must have known what he was going to do. I can't believe he didn't tell you.'

'I told you, I was dazed and confused.'

'Not so confused that you couldn't have found a way of stopping him.'

'I couldn't have stopped him, Kyle. I was quite ill—I was in hospital a few days. I wanted to contact you, but you didn't have a phone.'

'You could have asked someone to call me.'

'There was only my grandfather, and he...' She paused and wiped her eyes. 'It was several days before I was able to return home. As soon as I got to High Valley I went to the stables. I tried to find you, but you were gone.'

'There must have been *something* you could have done,' Kyle said grimly.

'There was nothing. And what about you, Kyle? Why did you never write to me? Never phone? I tried desperately to find out where you'd gone, but without success. I waited to hear from you— God, how I waited! I kept thinking you'd get in touch with me, but you never did.'

'Grant Dubois' granddaughter and the lowly stable-hand. To be honest, I didn't think you were interested any more.' His eyes were like dark holes—they seemed to have lost all their colour. 'You haven't told me, Liane, what did we have—boy or girl?'

'Don't do this to yourself, Kyle.'

'*Boy or girl*?'

'I don't know. I wish you wouldn't torture yourself like this. You're not doing yourself any good.' Liane's tone was heavy with pain—a pain she saw reflected in Kyle. His face was like a mask, very pale, with the skin stretched so tightly that it looked as if it might snap. His shoulders were rigid, and his hands were clenched into hard fists.

'I had a right to know,' he said then. 'I had a right to grieve. Your grandfather took those rights from me.'

'Kyle——'

'Did *you* grieve?' he demanded.

'I don't think I've ever stopped grieving,' she said simply.

'We should have done our grieving together, Liane. I'd have come to you in the hospital, and we'd have wept together. I'd have held you in my arms and kissed you, and we'd have comforted each other.'

Liane closed her eyes, and for a few moments she was able to see the picture Kyle's words evoked. And then she opened her eyes and saw the new Kyle, the man who was so different from the lad she'd once known.

'Now you know the whole story,' she said after a few seconds.

'I know the first part.'

'What do you mean?'

'Why didn't you tell me about it?'

She was puzzled. 'We've been over that—you'd left High Valley.'

'That was then. How about when I returned? You've had weeks in which to talk.'

'I couldn't...' She was trembling.

'We conceived a baby together, Liane, and you kept it from me. Whether you lost it or not, didn't you think I had a right to know?'

'I was going to tell you.'

'Were you really?' His voice was heavy with sarcasm.

'Yes!' she said.

'Why didn't you tell me the day I returned to High Valley?'

'I couldn't. Your arrival took me completely by surprise; I didn't know what to say.'

'And later? There were so many opportunities. When were you going to tell me? Before we were married? Afterwards? Or not at all?'

Liane looked into the eyes of the man she loved so much that without him there could be no life for her, and wished she knew a way to erase his pain.

'I was going to tell you when I felt the time was right,' she said honestly.

'I don't believe you.' The expression in his eyes echoed the contempt in his voice.

Abruptly, he stood up. Liane watched him pace around the room. On the floor near the door was a stack of pictures awaiting space on the walls of the house. One picture had slipped sideways; Kyle's shoe touched it, shifting it slightly, but he did not seem to notice.

'What now?' Liane asked.

He looked at her. 'I want you to leave.'

'Again?'

'I need to be alone. I have some thinking to do.'

Feeling numb, Liane stood up and walked towards the door. Her left hand was on the knob; she happened to glance at it. The ring... In a second, she knew what she had to do. She pulled the ring from her finger and held it out to Kyle.

'Take it,' she said.

He did not move, he just looked at her in silence.

'The ring, Kyle.'

'I don't want it.'

'Don't you understand? I'm giving it back to you.'

'Put it back on, Liane.'

'Why? There isn't going to be a wedding.'

'Did I say that?'

She stared at him. 'You just asked me to leave your house.'

'I didn't say the engagement was off.'

'You mean you still want to marry me?' she gasped.

'Yes.'

She looked at him uncomprehendingly a few seconds. Kyle was regarding her with such contempt, yet he still wanted her to be his wife. It did not make sense.

And then she understood.

'Of course you want to marry me,' she said bitterly. 'Now, more than ever, you have reason for revenge.'

'Remember that *you* said it, Liane, I didn't.'

She heard him give a short laugh as she wheeled out of the room and ran from the house.

CHAPTER EIGHT

'How do I look?' Liane turned from the mirror as her grandfather came into the room.

'Very beautiful.' Grant Dubois' voice was husky, and Liane thought she saw an unaccustomed moistness in his eyes. 'So like your mother on her wedding-day. I wish your parents could have seen you today, *liefie.*'

'I wish it too.'

Liane stood up, the folds of her long white dress billowing around her. Her grandfather held out his arms and she went into them. They held each other for a long moment, and she could feel the shuddering of his body.

'You've accepted Kyle, haven't you?' she asked, when he released her.

'If he's the man you love—and you say he is—then yes, I accept him. All I've ever wanted is your happiness, Liane.'

'Thank you, Gramps.'

'Perhaps I haven't always done the right thing.' His voice was troubled. 'Not telling Kyle you were pregnant, forcing him to leave High Valley. But at the time it seemed the only way.'

'I know that, and I don't blame you for what happened. You've always been good to me.'

They hugged each other again, then Grant Dubois said, 'Better stop this before we get too sentimental. The car's waiting outside—it's time we went, Liane.'

The wedding took place at High Valley, on the lawn outside the big house, where Liane had played as a child. It was one of those fine Cape days when the cloudless sky was a deep blue, the air was crisp and a stillness hung over the valley. The garden was at its best, the grass lushly green, all the flowers and shrubs in riotous bloom.

Liane walked across the lawn, one hand clamping her grandfather's arm, the other holding a bouquet of red roses and pink carnations and delicate baby's breath. With her arrival the pianist began to play the 'Bridal March', and the guests, who were sitting on folding chairs, rose to their feet.

Liane only registered the scene on the periphery of her mind, for her eyes were on one man, taller and more good-looking than anyone else, who stood watching her. His eyes were on her face as she walked slowly towards him, and her heart was so overflowing with love for him that she doubted she could hide her feelings.

And then she was standing beside him, and the wedding ceremony began. Listening to the minister speak the beautiful time-honoured words—'for richer, for poorer... in sickness and in health... till death do you part...'—Liane had to swallow the lump the words brought to her throat.

'Wilt thou have this woman to thy wedded wife?'

'I will.' Kyle said the words clearly and without hesitation.

'Wilt thou have this man to thy wedded husband?'

'I will,' she whispered.

And then Kyle was kissing her, and Liane closed her eyes and allowed herself to enjoy the moment.

'Liane,' he said softly, and she opened her eyes. She saw the hint of a smile on his lips, and an expression in his eyes, not quite affection, a little like tenderness. And that was strange, because Kyle had no tender feelings for her. In a moment the blood rushed to her cheeks, and she moved her eyes from his in confusion.

She was glad when the guests crowded around with their kisses and congratulations. Gramps, distinguished in his grey morning suit. Two aunts, her mother's sisters, who had travelled from the Transvaal for the wedding. Friends and neighbours, many of whom had been at Kyle's house-warming party.

'The evening you were Kyle's hostess, why didn't you tell us then that you two were going to be married?' asked one friend warmly.

'A Dubois back at High Valley—what could be more perfect?' said another.

'I'm so *relieved* Kyle didn't break off the engagement when he heard about the baby. I was *so* sure he knew about it, and afterwards, when I thought about his re-action, and realised he didn't know, I'd have done *anything* to take back what I said,' Elsbeth Barber whispered in her ear.

And Ted Lawrence, who had checked into the feasibility of re-zoning the fields beyond the fence, remarked in an undertone, 'So you married him, Liane. I wondered how you were going to get Kyle to change his mind about the development.'

Liane and Kyle were not alone together until the dancing began. To the strains of a slow waltz, the bridal couple took the floor.

'Well, Mrs Avery,' Kyle smiled down at her, 'you're a married woman now.'

'Married in name only,' she reminded him quietly.

'We exchanged vows.'

'Maybe we should have kept our fingers crossed, since we both know we don't intend keeping them.'

Kyle's eyes held Liane's a second longer, then she heard him laugh softly as he drew her against him, making conversation impossible. A few minutes later some of the guests began to dance too; Liane and Kyle could not have gone on talking even if they had wanted to.

All through the wedding reception Liane kept a smile on her face. Not for the world would she let anyone see that her heart was breaking because the day that should have been the happiest of her life was merely a charade. She smiled when the wedding-cake was cut; when she threw her bouquet in the direction of a favourite cousin; when Kyle—the picture of a loving bridegroom—kissed her. She smiled so much and so often that her face ached.

At last the guests began to go. Grant Dubois was the last to leave. Not usually a demonstrative man, he hugged Liane for the third time that day. 'Be happy, *liefie*,' he said gruffly. To Kyle he held out his hand, with a stern, 'Look after her.'

With her grandfather gone, Liane was free to abandon all pretence. She was alone with Kyle, her husband, and she was suddenly uneasy. The wedding was over—what now? Yesterday, at Kyle's urging, she had moved most of her possessions to High Valley. The house that had been her home most of her life was home again now. It made no sense that she should feel like a stranger with no idea what to do with herself.

As if he could read her thoughts, Kyle said, 'Why don't you change into something more comfortable?'

She darted him a suspicious look. 'Trousers and a blouse,' she told him crisply. If his thoughts ran to sexy underwear and transparent lingerie, the sooner she disabused him the better.

'Ideal,' he responded with a bland smile. 'I'm about to get out of these formal clothes myself too.'

Liane stopped in the doorway of the master bedroom, astonished to see jeans and a pink blouse laid out on the double bed, her favourite sandals on the carpet. It was as if Kyle had anticipated what she would want to wear. Overriding her objections, he had insisted she share the room with him; he had engaged a housekeeper who would think it odd if the newly married couple slept separately. Although Liane had understood that she had to give in on this point, she was not ready to get dressed in the same room as Kyle. Not when she did not feel married to him.

In a hurry suddenly to take off the dress that had seen her through the greatest acting performance of her life, she walked into the bathroom and took off the lovely white gown. Returning to the bedroom in the clothes Kyle had put out for her, she found him waiting for her. He too was casually dressed.

'Come,' he said.

'Where to?'

'You'll see.'

She followed him out of the room, out of the house. The silver car stood on the brick pad; the doors were open, and Kyle gestured to Liane to get in. Shrugging, she did as he said.

'Enjoy the wedding?' he asked, as they left High Valley.

'It went off well.'

'That wasn't my question.'

'What do you want me to say, Kyle? I knew we were both acting. At least, I don't think anyone else guessed the truth.'

Except for Ted Lawrence, and he knew the truth only because Liane had told him the lengths to which she would go in order to prevent the building of the farmers' mall. But Ted was a decent man. Unlike Elsbeth Barber, he would never divulge what he knew, would never utter poisonous words when the occasion suited him.

'Your grandfather was very civil,' Kyle remarked.

'Gramps has decided to accept our... our marriage. He told me again this morning that he was sorry for the things he did seven years ago.' Liane sat forward in her seat as Kyle took the car on to the highway. 'Where are we going?'

'I told you, you'll see. So your grandfather's sorry, is he?'

Glancing at him, Liane could see only his side-profile, but she knew him well enough to know that his expression would be hard.

'He *is* sorry,' she said in a low voice.

'Yes, Liane, I believe he is.'

She turned her eyes to the window. Kyle was driving fast. It was only when they had left the valley that it occurred to her that they were not just out for a post-wedding cooling-of-the-emotions drive.

She turned back to Kyle. 'Where *are* we going?' Suddenly it was important to have the question answered. 'I need to know.'

'All right, then—a little place I know on the Garden Route.'

'The *Garden Route*?' Her head jerked. 'But that's hours from here!'

He gave her an amused sideways glance. 'Why are you so surprised? Didn't you think we'd go on honeymoon?'

The question brought Liane a moment of pure joy, joy that reached into the very core of her being. A honeymoon! A time to be alone with Kyle. A time to repair his shattered trust, to show him how much she loved him. A time when, by some miracle, he might even grow to love her again too.

And then reality returned, and she said, 'Why?'

'Isn't this what bridal couples do?'

'Not when a wedding is a sham. Or is this just one more piece of the deception, Kyle? We've had all the others—the expensive engagement ring, the white dress, the lavish reception when a simple tea-party would have been enough. And now a honeymoon. Did you feel your revenge wouldn't be complete without one?'

'Do my motives matter?' he asked lazily.

'Yes, they do. Why didn't you tell me what you were planning?'

He grinned at her, and she said, 'I know the answer. You knew I'd refuse to go, so you kidnapped me instead.'

Kyle laughed, the sound so close to Liane, so vital and attractive, that she shivered.

'If I'd known we were going away, I'd have said something to my grandfather. He'll wonder where we are.'

'I've taken care of that,' he told her. 'He'll have been told by now.'

'And my job. They'll be expecting me at work tomorrow.'

'Taken care of too.'

'Just as well the wine-sellers' convention is over.'

'Just as well,' Kyle agreed.

Liane was struck by a new thought. 'I have nothing with me, none of my clothes apart from what I'm wearing now.'

'You won't need any clothes where we're going. We're honeymooners, Liane. You and I are married now.'

'Only for a short time,' she said unsteadily, wishing her heart didn't pound so hard at the thought of the days ahead.

'All the more reason to make the best of the time we do have together. Remember our toast the day we got engaged?'

Yes! Oh, yes! But she could not say the words. Shaken, Liane turned her head away, her eyes so blurred with tears that she could not see six inches beyond her window.

They stopped once for a meal, then hit the road again. Towards sunset Kyle turned the car off the main road and on to a bumpy track which seemed to end in a sand-dune, beyond which lay the ocean. To one side, almost invisible in the gathering darkness, Liane saw a tiny house.

'A fishing shack,' Kyle said, and she heard the smile in his voice. 'It belongs to a friend of mine. He's letting us use it for two weeks.'

'Two weeks without any clothes, off the beaten track. It will be——'

'An adventure—a romantic adventure.'

Even in the dim light Liane saw the wicked sparkle in Kyle's eyes, the glint of his teeth against his tan. A pirate, holding the heart of his kidnapped bride as bounty.

'Come,' he said, and she took the hand he reached out to her and walked with him to the shack.

It was more comfortable than it looked from the outside. Somebody must have been here quite recently, for it was swept and clean. In one corner there was a shelf holding all manner of fishing paraphernalia: nets and rods and hooks, heavy rubber boots and waterproof jackets. A fireplace was filled with logs, and on the floor in front of it was a bright woven rug. Beneath the window was a bed. Not quite a double bed, but bigger than a single one.

'Big enough for two,' Kyle said, his gaze following Liane's.

'I don't think so.'

'You'd be amazed how easily two can share a bed that size, Liane. How easily they can make love in it too.'

'That may be.' She tried to make her voice crisp. 'But a bed like that is for friends, not adversaries.'

'Are we adversaries, Liane?'

'We're a man and a woman playing at being married. We can't share that bed.'

'We'll talk about it later.'

'No, Kyle, there are things that need to be understood now. I know why we have to share a room at High Valley, but here, with nobody to pretend to——'

Kyle laughed the laugh that sent fire through Liane's veins every time she heard it. 'You're talking too much, my little bride.'

'But Kyle...'

He held out his hand to her. 'Let's wet our feet in the ocean before it's too dark.'

There was a voice inside her that warned her to resist him. But there was another voice too, a loud, treacherous, clamorous voice that said, Do as he says, enjoy this time together; you don't know when it will end.

And so she put her hand in his, and they walked out of the shack together. Evidently Kyle knew this place well, for he made his way surefootedly between two dunes and on to a small beach. They kicked off their sandals and walked to the edge of the water. The tide was in, the waves of the Indian Ocean rising, cresting, crashing on to the rocks and the sand with a deafening roar.

Kyle dropped Liane's hand and rolled up his jeans to the knee. When she had followed suit, they held hands once more and stepped into the foam of an outgoing wave. Another wave came in, the crashing water wetting Liane's hair and face with spray, and she put out her tongue and tasted salt on her lips, and laughed.

Kyle must have heard her laughter, because suddenly he was clasping her head in one hand, drawing back her wet hair with the other, and was laughing into her mouth. The salt on their lips mingled, and then the tip of his tongue touched hers, and desire was a hot torrent flooding her body. His arms went around her, drawing her against him, and she could no more have resisted him than she could have stopped herself breathing. The tide sucked the ocean floor from beneath their feet, but they did not move from their spot. Liane felt the strong thrusting of Kyle's legs, and as he went on kissing her her own legs leaned pliantly against his and the sound of her heartbeats blended with the roar of the waves.

They left the water eventually and began to make their way back to the shack. Kyle had left a light burning, and as they walked inside Liane had a sense of returning to a place she already knew and loved.

'Our clothes are soaked,' she said as he closed the door on a rising wind.

'So they are.'

'And we don't have others—at least, I don't.'

'Remember me telling you you won't be needing clothes here?'

'I can hardly spend two weeks in the same pair of jeans,' she protested. 'They'll be so stiff with salt in a day or two that they'll stand up straight by themselves.'

Kyle threw back his head and laughed. 'What a picture that would be. But you can always wash them and put them out in the sun to dry.'

'Wearing what, in the meantime?'

'How about your birthday suit?' His eyes sparkled with devilment.

'Come on, Kyle...'

'There's not another house within miles. Not a soul will see you, Liane.'

'Except you...'

'And I mean to see you anyway.'

She took a step away from him. 'No...'

'Naked and beautiful, just the way I remember you.'

'Don't,' she said painfully.

'You are my wife, Liane.' His voice was gruff. 'Remember the terms we agreed to——'

'The terms *you* laid out, sweetheart. I never agreed to them.'

She was taken aback, as much by the endearment as by the words. 'I told you how it would be between us. You never contradicted me.'

'I didn't agree with you either.'

'I took it for granted we understood each other.'

He laughed softly. 'That was a mistake.'

'But Kyle...we'll only be together a few years. And if we...' If we make love it will make it that much more difficult to part from you again, she wanted to say, but stopped herself. 'In the circumstances——' she began instead.

'In the circumstances, I intend to enjoy my wife as often as I possibly can.'

'We both know the ceremony today didn't mean anything.' He would never know how much it hurt her to say the words.

'Maybe not, but we put in a good performance all the same, didn't we? Everyone was fooled, including your grandfather. Now we can pretend to be on honeymoon. Who knows? We might even end up fooling ourselves.'

Kyle brushed his thumb along her cheek and down her throat, grinning with satisfaction when he heard the small hissing intake of her breath.

'One thing hasn't changed, Liane. We were always attracted to each other. We enjoyed each other's body seven years ago, and we still do today.' The stroking movement became more tantalising, more sensuous. 'You don't deny that, do you?'

She shook her head without speaking; in the light of all that had happened between them she would only sound absurd if she disagreed with him.

'Charade or not,' Kyle went on, 'I see no reason why we shouldn't make love whenever we choose. We even have a licence this time. We can't be hounded out of this place. Nobody will burst in on us and tell us to stop. We can do what we like, when we like. Perfect, isn't it?'

Quite perfect. Except that apart from the odd endearment Kyle had not spoken a single word of love or commitment. And without the words there could be no meaningful relationship for Liane.

She felt another brush-stroke down her throat. 'Let's pretend we're real honeymooners, Liane. That shouldn't be too difficult, should it? For starters, I'll make a fire, and after that we'll get out of our wet clothes.'

Liane watched him light the fire. She saw the twigs and bits of newspaper catch alight, and then the logs themselves. And all the white flames, white-hot and searing, were igniting within her own body, building into a fire that was impossible to contain.

Hunger gnawed at her loins, so that by the time Kyle turned from the hearth and came to her she could only look at him wordlessly. He began to unbutton her blouse. She put her hands over his, as if, even now, she felt some kind of protest was necessary, but Kyle said, 'Don't...' and she let her hands drop to her sides.

Kyle undressed her, first her blouse and bra and then her jeans, moving with a slowness that was almost unbearably sensuous, and all the while his eyes never left hers. At last she was naked. And now his eyes moved from her face to her body, lingering on her breasts before moving further to her hips and her long, slender thighs. After what seemed like eternity, his eyes lifted once more, and Liane saw that their expression had changed. The contained look was gone, and in its place was a smouldering passion.

'Undress me,' he ordered roughly.

Liane had never before undressed a man, but instinct told her what to do, and how. Like Kyle, she went slowly, teasing him, tantalising him, glorying in the urgency she sensed building inside him. Perhaps he would never love her in the way that she loved him, but it meant something to her that she could arouse and excite him.

'Who taught you to do that?' he asked hoarsely, when she had finished.

'Nobody.'

'*Sweetheart*!' he groaned. He reached out his arms to her, and as she went into them he pulled her hard against him. His lips against her ear, he whispered, 'You're not the girl I remember. You're a woman now—the sexiest woman I've ever known. Certainly the loveliest.'

He bent his head then and found her trembling mouth with his. Almost immediately their kisses turned from tenderness to passion. His hands slid over her, caressing the soft skin of her back and thighs, and at the same time her hands re-learned the feel of his body, the hard shoulders, the long spine and narrow hips—the body of a real man now, no longer a boy. Their arms wound around each other, their bodies straining, as if they could not get close enough, and Liane's excitement was akin to a physical ache.

'Come, darling,' Kyle said. Lifting her in his arms, he carried her to the fire. Gently he put her down on the rug, coaxing her into a lying position. Kneeling beside her, he began to caress her, brushing sensuously down her throat and then her breasts, cupping her nipples in his hands, breathing roughly as they grew hard beneath his fingers, stroking her hips and the soft skin of her inner thighs. And after he'd caressed her with his hands, he retraced the same path with his lips and tongue. A little moan escaped Liane, and she began to tremble with a desire that was unlike anything she had ever experienced—an elemental hunger, primitive and primeval.

By the time Kyle lowered himself on to her, she was just barely holding on to the last vestiges of sanity. Fulfilment, when it came, carried her to a peak of ecstasy that was beyond anything she had ever imagined.

They lay close together afterwards, still on the rug by the fire, and Liane was not aware of the moment when she fell asleep.

When she did wake up, she was puzzled by the unfamiliar texture beneath her back, by something heavy across her breasts. Opening her eyes, she was bewildered by the dimness and the smell of ash. It was a few moments before reality returned, and then it all came back to her—the fishing shack, the rug on the floor, the fire that had died some time during the night. The heaviness across her body was Kyle's arm.

She lay for a long while, revelling in his closeness, loving the slow sound of his breathing, the smell of him in her nostrils. Kyle Avery—her husband, her lover. And then she remembered the temporary nature of their relationship and a great sadness swept her. Their first separation had been hard enough, but to part from him after experiencing the bliss of marriage would be an agony she could not even begin to imagine. Somehow she must find a way of detaching herself from him at this point.

And that, she soon realised, was easier said than done.

Slowly, carefully, she lifted Kyle's arm away from her body. She was beginning to roll away from him when that arm folded around her once more and drew her close.

'Kyle...?' she whispered.

'Where are you going?'

'You're awake...'

'In more ways than one. I want to make love to you again.'

'It's morning and we should be getting up,' she said, as firmly as she could.

Kyle laughed as he lifted himself on one elbow and rubbed an unshaven cheek against her bare breast.

'Why on earth should we get up, Liane? We have no duties, no responsibilities. Nobody waiting for us, nobody expecting us. Nothing to do all day but enjoy ourselves.'

'Aren't you hungry? For something to eat,' she amended quickly as she saw fresh laughter in his face.

'We'll eat, Liane—after we've made love.'

He gathered her against him, and with his first kisses all her resolutions vanished. She was so deeply in love with Kyle that she had not the slightest wish to resist him.

The sun was high in the sky by the time they were ready for breakfast. Liane was surprised to find that Kyle had been to the shack a few days before their arrival, and had laid in a stock of food. They packed a basket with fruit and bread and a flask of coffee and took it to the beach. They ate on the rocks with the sun warming their bodies, and the waves licking their toes, and the gulls soaring overhead and squabbling over the scraps they threw them. They planned their day while they ate— swimming, sunbathing, scuba-diving, a walk along the beach. Interspersed with making love, Kyle said.

On their return to the shack, there was another surprise for Liane. Opening the boot of his car, Kyle brought out a suitcase packed with her clothes.

She danced him a smile. 'I admit to being impressed—you had this kidnapping arranged down to the last detail.'

The days merged one into the next, days of harmony and bliss. Liane and Kyle spent hours talking, catching up on the years they had missed. Only once did they talk about the baby they had lost.

'I still haven't got used to the idea that I could have been a father,' Kyle said one evening, as they sat on the rug in front of the fire.

'I think about it, too,' Liane said quietly.

For the most part, however, their talk was lighthearted, and every hour they spent together was enjoyable. They walked and swam and caught fish for their dinner. And every night they made love.

Liane had not known she could be so happy.

* * *

They had been married two weeks when they returned to High Valley. Liane left Kyle to unpack the car while she walked through the fields to the cottage. She saw her grandfather long before he saw her, dozing in his chair on the *stoep*, the bowl of his pipe overflowing with ash. He was looking frailer than ever.

Liane touched his cheek and said softly, 'Gramps...'

He murmured something indistinguishable, then his eyes fluttered open. 'Liane?' he said uncertainly.

'It's me, Gramps. We're back.'

'For a moment I thought I was dreaming, but it really is you, *liefie*.' A tremulous smile lit his face. 'Come here, child, and give your old grandfather a hug.'

When they had embraced, he said, 'That husband of yours treating you well?'

'Wonderfully.'

'I'm glad. It's good to have you back, Liane, even if this isn't your home any longer.'

The cottage would be her home again in time, but Liane made up her mind not to think about that until she had to.

'I couldn't be much nearer to you than High Valley,' she said briskly. 'I don't know if there's any food in the house today, but you'll come over for dinner tomorrow, Gramps.'

'That husband of yours may not want me.'

'I think he will. I'll come for you on my way back from the office.'

Her grandfather looked surprised. 'You're going back to work, Liane?'

'Of course. I've probably been away too long as it is.' She pulled up a chair beside his. 'Now tell me what you've been up to while I was away.'

Later that evening Kyle echoed Grant Dubois' words. 'You're going back to work, Liane?'

'Yes.'

'You don't have to, you know. I'm well able to support you.'

'That may be true—for the moment. But when our marriage ends I'll have to support myself again. I have a good job, Kyle; I might never find anything I like as much again.'

Kyle looked at her silently for a long moment, his eyes impersonal as they had not been since the wedding. 'You must do whatever you think is best, Liane,' he said.

CHAPTER NINE

LIANE and Kyle had been married almost two months when Liane began to suspect she might be pregnant.

She had ignored the first signs—a slight queasiness when she looked at certain foods, a feeling of weariness at times when she had, until then, been full of energy, an unusual tendency towards tears when she saw a movie that was even slightly sentimental. And then, one evening, the housekeeper put a dish of smoked *snoek* on the table. At the smell of the fish which had always been one of her favourites, Liane was swept with such nausea that she had to make a dash from the table.

Alone in her room, she sank down on the big double bed she shared with Kyle. When the heaving had stopped a thought struck her. Quickly she leafed through her diary, and an expression of wonder appeared in her face.

Early the next day she made an appointment with a doctor. A day after that, she asked for time off from work.

The doctor who examined her was a young woman, gentle and thorough, with an excellent reputation.

'Yes, Mrs Avery, I think you're pregnant,' she said at last, 'though I do need to run a test to be certain.'

Liane's eyes shone. 'A baby? I suspected . . . and yet— wow!—I can't quite take it in.'

'How long have you been married?' asked the doctor.

'Almost two months.'

'Your husband will be excited.'

The shine vanished from Liane's eyes. 'Maybe...'

'You seem uncertain.'

'I... I'm not sure my husband is ready to be a father.'

The doctor gave her a sympathetic look. 'Two months isn't long, and perhaps this has happened sooner than you both planned, but in my experience husbands are usually nearly as thrilled as their wives.'

Normal husbands. Men who expected their marriages to last. Men who loved their wives...

'There's a restaurant on the next corner—why don't you go and have a cup of tea?' the doctor said. 'If you come back in an hour or so, I'll be able to let you know the result of the test.'

Liane decided to do as the doctor had suggested. She had noticed the restaurant on her way in, and she was relieved to find a free table by a window, well away from a party of smokers; in her fragile state, smoke could only add to her discomfort.

A waitress came to the table, and Liane asked for a pot of tea and a slice of unbuttered toast—it was as much as she felt able to handle.

She stared out of the window, but her eyes were unfocused. She did not see the traffic, or the people, or the woman walking past the restaurant with two miniature poodles, little red bows around their necks and obviously fresh from a grooming parlour.

A baby... Perhaps, at last, the void that had been in her heart since the day of her miscarriage would be filled.

Kyle... The thought of telling him the news made her tremble.

She drained her cup and poured another. Although she found she could not touch the toast after all, the tea was welcome. She finished the second cup and glanced at her watch. It was time to return to the doctor. Catching the waitress's eye, she asked for her bill.

As Liane had guessed it would be, the test was positive, and at the doctor's suggestion she made an appointment to see her again a month later.

She returned to the winery, but she found it hard to concentrate on her work; disciplined as she was, it was impossible to prevent her mind from wandering to Kyle and the baby. An envelope arrived on her desk, an unofficial letter from the president of the winery, congratulating her on the success of the wine-sellers' convention, but Liane merely skimmed it before putting it in a folder with other similar letters.

She was relieved when the day came to an end and she was free to leave the office. Driving up to the farmhouse, she saw that the brick pad was empty. Kyle was nowhere in sight; Anna, the housekeeper, said he had left the farm early that morning without saying what time he would be back.

Declining Anna's offer of something to eat, Liane went to her room, where she changed out of her city clothes before stepping into the shower. After she had towelled herself dry, she studied her body in the mirror. There was no change in her figure—not yet. Soon there would be.

When she had put on a shirt and a pair of shorts, she lay down on the bed. From the kitchen, where Anna was preparing dinner, came the sounds of saucepans being moved about. Closing her eyes, Liane wondered briefly whether she was going to be able to cope with eating a meal.

And then her thoughts went to Kyle. So much depended on his reaction to the news. Would he resent the unexpected intrusion into a marriage that had never been intended to last? Or would he suggest that they put aside their feelings and remain together for the sake of their baby? And what of her own feelings? Could she bear to live with a man, year after year, deeply in love with him, yet knowing that his only motive for marrying her had been one of revenge, and that any attraction she had for him was purely physical? It was a question that needed little thought; the happiness of their child was more important than anything else. And perhaps, in time, Kyle might even come to love her...

Suddenly, through the open window, she heard the familiar sound of a car coming up the drive. Determined that Kyle should not find her on the bed, she got up quickly, splashed her face with water and ran a comb through her hair. She was at the front door by the time Kyle came up the steps.

'Hi. Got home before I did, did you?' He looked happy to see her.

'Anna said you'd been out all day,' Liane told him.

'I've been busy.' He cupped her face in his hands and kissed her lightly on the lips. 'I don't know if dinner's ready, but I'd love to relax in the garden for a while before we eat. Would that upset Anna very much, do you think? No? Great! I'm dying for a beer. Will you have one too, Liane?'

'Not today, thanks.'

'Sure?'

'Quite, though a fruit juice would be lovely.'

He stopped her as she was about to go indoors. 'I'm going inside anyway; I'll bring out our drinks.'

Kyle took off his jacket, slinging it over his shoulder as he walked through the door. Liane crossed the lawn to a group of wooden chairs in the shade of an oak tree that was as old as High Valley itself. A few minutes later Kyle emerged from the house carrying a tray. Married life, Liane thought. In other circumstances, how much I'd enjoy it!

She waited until Kyle had taken a sip of his beer, then said, 'I have some news. I——'

'There's something I need to tell you, Liane.'

'But Kyle, I——'

'I have to go away for a few days.'

Kyle's eyes had a distant look, as if he was so absorbed in his thoughts that he had not taken in Liane's own efforts to talk.

'Where are you going?' she asked after a moment.

'Up north.'

'Business trip?'

'Yes.'

'But they've been coping so well there without you,' protested Liane. 'What with your computer and the fax machine, you've been in constant touch with your office all the time.'

'True. Things have been going very well, although it's time I set up a proper office here too. But something's come up, Liane. I won't bore you with all the details, but it's urgent, and I'm needed there right away.'

'When will you leave?'

'I'm catching the first plane out tomorrow morning. I should really have left today, but it wasn't possible. Besides, I didn't want to go without telling you.'

'How long will you be away?'

'A few days. No more than a week at the most, I hope. You'll be able to cope here alone, won't you?'

She gave him a dry look. 'Have you forgotten that High Valley was my home long before I married you?'

He leaned across to touch her cheek, his fingers cool from his glass. 'Absurd question, I agree. Put it down to intense preoccupation.'

She smiled at him. 'You're forgiven.'

He took another sip of his beer. Then he said, 'I have a feeling I interrupted you—there was something you wanted to tell me.'

'There still is, but it'll keep till you get back.'

'Sure?'

'Quite.'

With Kyle's thoughts obviously elsewhere, this was not the right time to tell him about the baby. It was important for Liane to know she had his undivided attention when she told him the news. In the circumstances, it was best to wait for his return.

'Nothing planned for this evening, I hope?' he asked.

'Not a thing.'

'Good,' Kyle drawled lazily, 'because I have plans of my own.'

As Liane recognised the expression which had appeared in his eyes, a shiver of desire flamed inside her. She managed to dance him an innocent look. 'What kind of plans?'

'I want to make love to my wife tonight. Wild, passionate love.'

The desire increased. 'Don't you have things to do before you leave tomorrow?'

'I do, but they won't take me all evening. When I'm finished at my desk I want to make love to you—lovemaking that will sustain me for all the days I'll be away from you.'

The look in Kyle's eyes was as sensuous as a caress. He reached for Liane's hand, giving the palm a swift seductive lick before pressing his lips to it.

'Will you let me make love to you all night, Liane?'

'Yes,' she whispered.

Tonight they would make love. Tomorrow Kyle would leave High Valley. When he returned she would tell him about the baby.

Liane had not realised she would miss Kyle quite as much as she did. The double bed, where they had made such abandoned love the night before his departure, now seemed very big, very empty. She would move across the bed during the night, unconsciously seeking the warmth of her husband's body, and when she touched nothing but sheets and blankets she would wake up to a feeling of immense disappointment. How long until Kyle was a vibrant presence in her bed once more?

Her hours in the winery were busy, making the days bearable, and often on the way home from work she would spend some time with her grandfather, having dinner with him before driving home. It was when she was alone at High Valley that she missed Kyle the most. He phoned her several times, but not every night, and there was many an evening when she went to bed disappointed at not hearing from him.

Late one afternoon Liane returned to High Valley to find the sleek silver car on the brick pad. Kyle! In seconds her heartbeat doubled. Slamming on the brakes, she leaped from the car. The door of the house was open, and she ran inside calling, 'Kyle . . . ?'

The door of the library opened, and there he was, eyes sparkling, hair a little dishevelled, teeth white against his tan—even more ruggedly handsome than she'd visualised him at night in bed. And so very sexy.

Will our child look like you, Kyle? she thought suddenly.

'Liane . . .' He held out his arms to her.

'Why didn't you tell me you were coming?' she asked when he'd kissed her.

'Because I didn't know myself until early today. Things sorted themselves out fairly suddenly. I just rang the airways and was lucky to get a flight.'

'I'd have fetched you from the airport,' she told him.

'I'd left my car in the city—remember?' He was laughing down at her. 'I think I took Anna by surprise too. She looked amazed when I walked in. No food in the house for dinner tonight, I suppose?'

'Serve you right if there wasn't,' Liane teased back. 'Actually, I've been having dinner with my grandfather most days, but maybe, just maybe, we'll dredge up something for you to eat.'

'If not, we'll go out somewhere.' He put his arms around her and held her tight. 'It's good to see you, Liane.'

It was utter bliss to see him, but Liane contented herself with reciprocating the compliment. 'Good to see you too,' she said softly. 'And I was only teasing you, Kyle. We'll eat at home. And afterwards...'

They would have the special candle-lit dinner she'd been planning since the moment she'd known about the pregnancy. Afterwards she would tell him the news there had been no time to tell him before he'd gone off on his trip. 'And afterwards I have something to tell you...' Those were the words she was starting to say, but the sentence died on her lips as a second person walked out of the library.

A stranger. A woman. Late twenties, tall and slim and very beautiful, with short dark hair, glossy and beautifully cut, framing her striking face, wearing a scarlet trouser-suit which showed off her gorgeous figure to perfection.

Kyle's arms dropped away from Liane as he turned to the woman, who had stepped forward and was saying, 'Are you going to introduce me?'

'Of course. My wife, Liane. Liane, this is Ingrid Macy.'

Ingrid held out her hand. 'Hello, Liane. I'm glad to meet you; I've heard a lot about you from Kyle.' Her smile was self-assured, her demeanour sophisticated, mirroring none of Liane's own sense of confusion.

'I'm glad to meet you too, Ingrid.' Liane hid her feelings with a smile of her own. 'Are you a relative of Kyle's, or a friend? I'm sorry, I don't mean to sound ignorant...'

'Ingrid is my secretary,' said Kyle. 'We've been working together all week, but there's other work left to do, and I suggested she come out here for a while. I told her she could stay at High Valley.'

'Yes, of course,' Liane said, a little too quickly, a little too brightly.

'Won't be a problem, will it?' Ingrid was watching her.

'No, of course not.'

'I mean, normally I wouldn't dream of intruding on a newly married couple.'

Liane saw that Kyle was watching her too now, his expression hard to read, and for a moment she wondered if he had told Ingrid that Liane's own stay at High Valley was only temporary.

Calling upon centuries of Dubois hospitality and tradition, she gave Ingrid another smile. 'You mustn't feel you're intruding; you're very welcome in our home. Kyle's been teasing me about food—I think I should go and talk to Anna about dinner.'

An hour later they sat down to their meal, and Ingrid was visibly impressed with her surroundings.

'This is wonderful.' Her voice had a seductive quality, Liane thought. 'All the things you used to tell me about High Valley, Kyle—I used to think you must be exaggerating, but you weren't. It's all true.'

How long had Kyle known this very attractive woman? And how well? Liane made herself very busy dishing up the food, so that the other two would not see the questions in her eyes.

But they were not looking at her at all. Kyle was saying to Ingrid, 'Maybe now you can understand why I had to come back here?'

'Oh, yes, I understand,' smiled Ingrid.

'There's a lot you haven't seen yet. Tomorrow Liane and I will show you the stables.'

'Where your life began. Amazing, Kyle, I can never think of you as a stable-boy. A case of mimbo-dimbo, I suppose?'

'Precisely,' Kyle said, and they both burst out laughing.

At the risk of appearing foolish, Liane echoed, 'Mimbo-dimbo?'

Ingrid stopped laughing. 'A private joke. We could tell you about it—couldn't we, Kyle?—but it would take an age and you'd probably be bored.'

'Ingrid's right.' At least Kyle had the grace to look contrite. 'You'd be thoroughly bored, Liane; it's a story that goes way back and really isn't worth telling. But no more jokes like that in front of Liane, if you don't mind, Ingrid. She can't possibly think they're funny.'

When they had finished eating, they moved outside to the veranda. Kyle and Ingrid began to talk about a movie they had both seen, their conversation so lively that they seemed not to notice that Liane took little part in it. Ingrid cracked another coded joke, but this time Liane did not question it, and there was no reproach from Kyle.

Liane was glad her face was in shadow, so that she did not have to smile for the purpose of pretending an amusement she was far from feeling. Private jokes... The words, with their connotation of intimacy, brought thoughts and questions she would have liked to push from her mind. One question was uppermost and difficult to ignore: apart from being Kyle's secretary, what other role had Ingrid Macy played in his life?

The evening wore on. Until her pregnancy, Liane had always been full of energy, but now she tired easily. Kyle and Ingrid showed no signs of weariness, but there came a moment when Liane could no longer sit upright.

She got to her feet. 'Will you excuse me? It's been a long day...'

Kyle reached for her hand and gave it a quick squeeze. 'I'll be along soon.'

'I'll be waiting for you,' she said lightly.

And she would be, Liane decided, as she began to get ready for bed. All week she had been longing to be alone with Kyle. She could not wait to feel his arms around her, to enjoy his kisses and caresses. There had been an urgency in his arms earlier, when they'd embraced, that said he too was looking forward to their lovemaking.

Afterwards, when they lay together in the aftermath of love, she would tell him about the baby.

She put on her prettiest négligé. There was a perfume Kyle particularly liked, and she dabbed a little behind her ears and between her breasts. She switched off the ceiling light, so that the only light in the room was the glow from the reading-lamp beside the bed. Through the open window she heard the sound of voices, the words indistinguishable, and the low cadence of shared laughter. To keep herself awake, Liane picked up the book she'd been reading all week—a thriller. But she was even more tired than she'd realised. She closed her eyes—just for a few seconds, she told herself—and she did not know it when the book dropped from her hands and her head rolled sideways on the pillow.

She did not hear Kyle walk into the room. She did not see his look of disappointment, or the way he stood by the bed looking down at her, a rueful smile lifting his lips. She did not react when he put her book on the table and switched off the light. She did not stir when he bent and kissed her, very lightly, first on her cheeks and then on her lips.

The smell of bacon hit Liane as she was walking towards the dining-room the next morning. Nausea gripped her instantly. No breakfast for her today, she decided, not even coffee.

In the doorway of the dining-room she stopped. The sun was streaming through the east-facing windows on to the table where Kyle and Ingrid were sitting, their heads close together, so engrossed in their conversation that they were not aware of Liane's presence. Ingrid said something in that seductive voice of hers, and Kyle put his hand over hers and laughed.

Pain shot through Liane, knifing her beneath her ribs. When she could speak, she said lightly, 'Good morning...'

The two heads swung round, then Kyle said, 'Liane, hi, we started breakfast without you—come and join us.'

'Actually, I'm just on my way out.'

'Without eating?' Ingrid asked curiously.

This morning Ingrid was wearing a pale blue sundress with a cleavage that revealed the top of her breasts, and straps that were so narrow that her smoothly tanned shoulders looked bare. She looked anything but a secretary ready to embark on hours of serious work, Liane thought, glancing down at her own no-nonsense skirt and jacket.

'I'm going to give breakfast a skip today,' she said.

'But you never go without eating,' Kyle protested. 'Sit down and have a cup of coffee with us before you leave.'

Liane knew she could not sit down at the table. Not until the nausea wore off, which it would in an hour or two. She took a step backwards. 'Actually, I'm a little late. Have a good day, and I'll see you both later.'

It was only when she had passed three fast-moving vehicles that she realised she was driving much too fast herself. A little grimly, she put her foot on the brakes and slowed the car. She could *not* let herself think about Kyle and Ingrid—seductively beautiful Ingrid—closeted cosily together in the library all day; she would only torture herself if she did.

Late that afternoon they sat together on the veranda before dinner, and Kyle asked the two women what they wanted to drink.

'Nothing for me, thanks,' Liane said.

'Ingrid?'

'Whatever catches your eye.' She laughed up at him. 'You've always known what I like, Kyle.'

When Kyle had gone inside, Ingrid turned to Liane. 'What a glorious place this is. It must have been wonderful for you to grow up here.'

'It was heaven,' Liane agreed.

'Kyle has told me so much about High Valley over the years,' Ingrid went on. 'He wouldn't have seen it from your perspective, of course, but he loved it too.'

'Which is why he bought it when he had the chance. One of the reasons, anyway.'

Did Ingrid know the real reason why Kyle had returned to the farm? How much had he told her? Liane wished she had a way of knowing.

'I have to keep reminding myself that I'm here to work,' Ingrid said. 'Being here feels much more like a holiday.'

'How long will you be here?' Liane kept her voice neutral.

'About a week.'

A week was bearable. A week she could handle. Her eyes on the distant mountains, she said, 'I gather you've known Kyle for quite a while?'

'A few years. Three, to be exact.' Ingrid's tone had a dry note.

'And you've been his secretary all that time?'

'No, not all of it. There was a time when we were just friends.'

'I see...'

In that same dry tone, Ingrid said, 'That is what you're asking, isn't it?'

Liane turned a flushed face. 'Can you blame me for being curious? Kyle and I haven't been married long, and although we were close long ago there's so much I don't know about his recent past.' She paused a moment, then summoned her courage and went on. 'And the two of you seem to know each other well.'

'I guess that's obvious. All right, Liane, we were very good friends. For a while I even thought we might... But there you are, he married you instead. That should be enough for you.'

'It is,' Liane said, with a conviction she was far from feeling. She was glad when Kyle returned to the veranda moments later, making further intimate conversation impossible.

She did not tell Kyle about the baby that night. One week and Ingrid would be gone from High Valley. She and Kyle would have the house to themselves once more. She would tell him then.

Morning light streamed into the room, and Liane sat up with a start. Glancing at her watch, she saw that it was almost eight o'clock. She should have been up at least an hour ago—she would be late for work!

She was getting out of bed when she remembered it was Saturday. Remembered too the restless night she had spent, for she had woken during the early hours feeling uncomfortable, and for a while she had been unable to get back to sleep. No wonder she had slept longer today.

As she lay back against the pillows, stretching her body lazily beneath the sheets, she remembered something else. Ingrid was leaving today.

Suddenly there was everything to get up for. Kyle was driving Ingrid to the city, where she would catch her plane, and Liane would go with them. When they had dropped Ingrid at the airport, they would spend a lovely day on the beach, dance and dine perhaps at a favourite restaurant, after which they would drive back to the valley. Later, in bed, she would tell him about the baby.

Liane gave a laugh of pure happiness as she threw aside the blankets and got quickly out of bed. She opened her wardrobe and took out a pair of pink and white striped culottes and a matching pink blouse. The culottes had an elastic waistband, which was just as well; she could still get into most of her clothes, but a few were beginning to feel a bit tight.

She went into the bathroom and let the water run in the bath. And then she walked back into the bedroom and flung open the window. She was leaning out, breathing in the sparkling morning air, when she saw two people walking towards a clump of high shrubs on the far side of the lawn. Kyle and Ingrid, deep in conversation. On this day of Ingrid's departure Liane no longer felt threatened by the woman who had once been Kyle's very good friend.

She was about to call a hello to them when she saw them stop. Ingrid looked up at Kyle; she seemed to be saying something to him. A moment later his hands went to her face, then he was drawing her to him. Their arms went around each other, and their heads came together for a kiss.

Liane did not wait to see how long they kissed, or how passionately. Blindly she wheeled away from the window. Sinking down on her bed, she put her hands over her eyes. Kyle and Ingrid . . . A relationship that had not dissolved with Kyle's marriage to Liane, that was merely waiting in the wings until the charade of his present marriage ended. How stupid, how *incredibly* stupid she had been to let herself believe otherwise.

The sound of water intruded on her thoughts. When she had switched off the taps, she returned to the room. Her eyes fell on the cheerful culottes and blouse she'd laid out on a chair, and she shoved them back in her wardrobe and took out jeans and a T-shirt instead; down-to-earth clothes, infinitely drabber.

She was dressed and brushing her hair when Kyle walked in. He was looking particularly handsome this morning, Liane noticed with a heavy heart. As he came over to her and kissed her lightly on the lips, she made herself very still. He stood back then and stared down at her in surprise. 'This is what you're wearing today?'

She gave him a steady look. 'Anything wrong with it?'

'For a day at High Valley it would be fine. Did you forget Ingrid is leaving today?'

Liane shook her head.

'And you are going to spend the day in the city?'

'I'm not going with you, Kyle,' she said flatly.

He pushed a hand through his hair. 'I don't understand—we'd made plans.'

'I have other plans now.'

'Does it mean nothing that I was looking forward to spending our first day alone together again with you?' Kyle's lips had set in a tight line and his expression was hard.

Liane put down her brush and stood up. Her throat was thick with tears, but she managed to swallow them before she answered. 'I'm sorry,' she said, as lightly as she could.

'Ingrid will be surprised.'

'I think she'll get over it. I'll say goodbye to her here, before she leaves.'

She flinched as Kyle gripped her shoulders. 'What are you playing at?'

'Am I playing?'

'We're married, Liane.'

'In name only,' she reminded him evenly.

Kyle held her a moment longer. 'Have it your own way,' he said then, and strode out of the room.

CHAPTER TEN

AN HOUR later Liane said goodbye to Ingrid.

The other woman had never looked quite as beautiful as she did today, Liane thought. Her eyes shone and there was a radiance in her face. No wonder Kyle was in love with her. A man would find it very difficult not to be affected by Ingrid's loveliness.

'Are you going to change your mind and come along for the drive, Liane?' Ingrid asked.

Liane saw that Kyle was watching her, his eyes impersonal, revealing nothing of his thoughts.

'I have things to do here,' she said quietly.

Ingrid thanked Liane for her hospitality, then Kyle said, 'Time to go.' Without another look at Liane, he opened the door for his secretary.

When the car was out of sight, Liane went back into the house. She put two suitcases on her bed, opened her wardrobe and began to take out her clothes. Tears spilled out of her eyes and on to her cheeks as she began to pack.

Anna was in the kitchen with the door closed when Liane carried first one case, then the other, out to the car, and Liane was glad. Fond as she was of Anna, she could not tell the housekeeper her plans before she had spoken to Kyle. In a day or two she would phone Anna, thank her for all her kindness, and say a proper goodbye.

Grant Dubois was still in bed, and astonished to see her when she walked into the cottage. 'What on earth are you doing here?' he asked.

'Don't I visit you most days, Gramps?'

'Never so early on a weekend morning. I'd have thought you two love-birds would be busy doing whatever it is newly-weds do when they have some time together.'

Liane felt fresh tears rising to her eyes. 'Well, as you see, I'm here,' she said, as briskly as she could. 'Say, Gramps, why don't you get up—no, you don't need to get dressed first—and I'll make us some breakfast?'

Despite her morning sickness, she was glad to escape to the kitchen before the tears could flow once more. It wouldn't do to cry in front of her grandfather, who would ask her questions which she was not yet ready to answer. Time for that later, when she could trust herself to talk without breaking down.

When she had put the coffee on to brew, she put two slices of bread in the toaster, and forced herself to make an omelette the way her grandfather liked it. By the time he joined her in the kitchen, his meal was waiting for him, and Liane had regained some small semblance of control.

They sat together at the round table, Grant Dubois eating the meal which Liane had prepared for him, Liane confining herself to a cup of weak tea, and it was a bit like the old days, when they had always eaten together. Except that everything had changed. She was married, and her husband had no idea that she'd left him, and her grandfather did not know yet that she was moving back in with him.

'Kyle busy around the farm?' Grant Dubois asked after he had finished his meal.

'He's gone into the city.'

'Didn't know the man works on weekends.'

'He's driving his secretary to the airport—the woman who's been staying with us—Ingrid Macy.'

'Didn't you want to go along?' asked Grant.

Liane began to stack the dishes. 'Not particularly.'

'You could have made a day of it together.'

'We could have, but I didn't want to.'

Her grandfather shot her a quick, curious look. Then he stood up, thanked her for breakfast, and said he was going off to get dressed.

Ignoring her queasiness, Liane washed the dishes and tidied the kitchen. When she had finished, she went out to the *stoep*. Not long afterwards her grandfather joined her. For a while they sat together in silence, Grant Dubois puffing on his pipe, Liane with her eyes glued to a magazine which she was just pretending to read.

Only when she felt that she could talk without crying did she say, 'If it's OK with you, I'd like to stay here tonight.'

'Just tonight?' He did not sound as surprised as he might have.

'Not just tonight, Gramps.'

'How many nights are we talking about, Liane?'

'A few.'

'Two? Three?'

'More than that.'

'I see.'

Silence again, while Liane swallowed on the lump in her throat. A few minutes had passed when she spoke again. 'Well—is it OK with you, Gramps?'

It was Grant Dubois' turn to be silent now. Puffing on his pipe, he looked across the fields. Liane began to feel tense.

'People change, Liane,' he said eventually. 'They grow older, hopefully they become a little wiser. Just when they think they know it all they realise they never knew it at all.'

'Profound thoughts,' she tried to say lightly.

'I'm trying to tell you that I've been wrong about certain matters.'

'Oh?'

'I don't have to tell you how furious I was when Kyle came back into your life,' said Grant. 'When you said you were going to marry him I was devastated. Liane... *Liefie*, are you listening to me?'

'I'm wondering why you haven't said whether I can stay.'

'I'm a stubborn old codger, and it isn't easy for me to say these things, but I was wrong about Kyle.'

'Gramps——' Liane put out her hand, wanting to stop the flow of words.

But her grandfather went on anyway. 'I've come to respect him, Liane. He isn't the scoundrel I used to think he was. Kyle Avery is a good, strong man. In many ways he reminds me of his father. He's the right man for High Valley. And I believe now that he's the right man for you as well.'

She turned to him without caring that her expression was distraught. 'Why are you telling me all this? Why *now*?'

'Something's happened—that's obvious.'

'Gramps——'

'A lovers' quarrel? I don't want to hear about it, child. I don't want to be put in the position of having to give you advice. And I want you to know that I like your husband.'

There was nothing Liane could say to that. And her grandfather, puffing on his pipe as he stroked his dog, did not seem to expect an answer.

Kyle drove up a few hours later. Liane had known he would come. Watching the man she loved so much walking towards the cottage, she wished there was a way of making a clean break with him. Unfortunately, that would be impossible. As the father of her baby, Kyle would insist on playing his part in the child's life, and Liane knew she would not have it otherwise. She wanted her child to have a father. Yet the thought of having to see Kyle, month after month, year after year, probably with Ingrid Macy at his side, was incredibly painful.

By the time he strode up the steps to the *stoep*, every muscle in her body had tightened.

There were no polite preliminaries as he stopped abruptly in front of her. 'We have to talk, Liane.'

Liane's grandfather rose to his feet. 'I'll go inside.'

'You don't have to do that, Gramps,' pleaded Liane.

Grant Dubois looked from one ashen face to the other. 'I think it's best,' he said, and went into the house.

'You didn't even have the guts to tell me you were leaving,' snapped Kyle.

'I didn't know myself until this morning,' Liane explained. 'And I could hardly tell you in front of Ingrid.'

'How do you think I felt when I got back to High Valley and found you gone? Without so much as a note or a word?'

'I'm sorry, it was the only way I could do it,' she said faintly.

'We are married, Liane.'

'Are we?'

'Yes, dammit, we are! And while you're my wife I expect you to live with me.'

'Even though our marriage is a charade?' she taunted him.

'It was always based on certain terms. Your terms, Liane.'

'It was never intended to be permanent.'

'You spoke of years. A few *years*, Liane. Why do you want to leave me now, after less than three months?'

She looked at him uncertainly. 'I didn't realise how difficult it would be to live together.'

'Is it so difficult?' he asked.

'Yes.'

His eyes were bleak. After a moment he said, 'You should have thought of that when you asked me to marry you.'

'You know why I did that.'

'Yes,' he said flatly. 'I do know.'

Liane saw his eyes go to the fields beyond the fence.

'Are you saying that if I don't return to you you'll go ahead with the farmers' mall?' she whispered.

Kyle looked at her silently. His hands had been shoved deep into the pockets of his trousers, his feet were planted squarely on the stone floor of the *stoep*. He had the inflexible look of a man with whom it would be impossible to argue.

'You'd really go ahead and build that mall, Kyle?' she persisted.

Still he was silent.

'Why don't you answer me?' Liane demanded.

'What's the point? You seem to know all the answers. You always have, haven't you?'

They stood staring at each other, like two combatants who had never shared tenderness or passion, who had never slept together in one bed.

'I'll go inside and fetch your suitcases,' Kyle said harshly.

'Don't bother. They're still in my car.' Liane felt ill.

'No need to waste time, then. Let's go, Liane; I told Anna we'd be home in time for dinner.'

Dinner was a grim and silent meal, served by a very nervous-looking housekeeper. Kyle did not do Anna's good cooking justice, Liane noticed abstractedly; she herself only played with the food on her plate.

After the meal she went directly to their bedroom. Her suitcases were still on the double bed where Kyle had dropped them. The door of the wardrobe was ajar, as

Kyle must have left it after he'd come home and found her gone.

Slowly, reluctantly, Liane unpacked her clothes and put them back on hangers and in drawers. She put out her brushes on the dressing-table, and her cosmetics and toiletries in the bathroom. When she had finished she glanced at her watch. It was still quite early, much too early for bed. A long evening stretched ahead of her.

There would be many such evenings in the future.

She left the room. Anna was no longer in the kitchen, and Kyle, mercifully, was nowhere in sight. Liane went to the library and picked up the thriller she'd begun to read a week earlier. She had been staring sightlessly at the same page for at least an hour when Kyle walked into the room.

'Harmonious picture,' he commented.

Liane looked up tensely. Kyle was close to her chair, towering about her in a way that made the room seem too small.

'I'm enjoying my book,' she tried to say lightly.

'I want to enjoy my wife.'

The breath caught in her throat. 'No!'

He reached for her hands, jerking her to her feet.

'Anna...' Liane protested.

'Anna isn't here. We're alone, Liane.'

'That may be, but——'

'We haven't made love since Ingrid arrived.'

'You can't blame me for that,' Liane protested over the wild clamouring of her senses. 'In any case——'

'You're talking a darn sight too much,' he said roughly, and pulled her into his arms. And then he was kissing her, so hungrily, so passionately that she was a little frightened. Without taking his mouth from hers, he tore off her blouse and his shirt. And then they were holding each other so feverishly, so tightly that the frantic beat of his heart coincided with the thud of the pulse in her throat.

After a while, he held her a little away from him so that he could look down at her, and she shuddered when she saw the passion in his eyes.

'You're so beautiful!' His voice was thick. 'There's a new ripeness in your body. Your breasts, darling, were they always so full, so sexy?'

She stared at him, unable to speak.

'I can't be patient, Liane, not tonight. Where do you want to make love? Here, on the floor? Or in bed?'

'Kyle——'

'Where, Liane? Tell me quickly!'

From nowhere, Ingrid's face came into Liane's mind. Once more she saw Kyle and Ingrid in the garden, their arms around each other.

She gave a violent shake of the head. 'Nowhere.'

He tried to reach for her again, but she pushed herself out of his arms. She was shivering uncontrollably now. 'Leave me alone, Kyle.'

'You can't be serious! You want it too.'

'No, I don't want to go on with this.'

'Darling, please...' He tried to lift her into his arms, but she made herself rigid.

'This isn't lovemaking, it's just a farce.'

'Our passion is real, Liane.'

'That's all you want me for—my body.'

'You enjoy it as much as I do.' His breathing was ragged, but his voice was hard. 'And don't pretend you don't, because we'd both know you were lying.'

'I won't pretend.' Liane's eyes were filled with tears. 'I do enjoy it, I can't deny that. But afterwards... I have to live with myself afterwards, Kyle. And then I feel used and cheap.'

'We're married,' he insisted.

Painfully, she shook her head. 'What we have isn't a marriage.'

He stepped away from her abruptly, and the contempt in his face was so intense that she flinched.

'You have to understand...' she began despairingly.

'I understand that you disgust me,' he said harshly, then picked up his shirt and strode from the room.

'Mrs Avery?'

'Yes?'

'Liane Avery?'

'Yes, who is this?'

'It's the hospital. I'm afraid there's been——'

'What's happened?' gasped Liane.

'There's been an accident, and——'

'An *accident*?' The colour drained from Liane's cheeks in an instant. 'Where? What's happened? My husband... Is it Kyle?'

'There was a fire at your grandfather's cottage.' The unfamiliar voice at the other end of the line was sympathetic.

'*Gramps*? Is he all right? Don't tell me he's——'

'He's fine, Mrs Avery. Or he will be when he's had some attention.'

'Thank God!'

'Your husband is in slightly worse shape, I'm afraid,' the voice went on.

'My husband? *Kyle*? What are you saying?'

'He was there at the time, but he'll be fine too, the doctors say.'

'Oh, God!' The words emerged on a sob.

'Can you get to the hospital, Mrs Avery? Better still, can you get someone to drive you here?'

Liane was already on her feet, her free hand knocking down a stack of folders from her desk. She did not stop to pick them up as she cried into the phone, 'I'll be there immediately!' and ran out of the room.

She would have driven herself. She was, in fact, on her way out of the winery when one of the directors saw her in the car park, registered her shock, took her by the arm and insisted on leading her to his car.

In minutes they were at the hospital. Not long after that Liane was speaking to a nurse in the emergency department. She could see her grandfather, she was told. It would be a while longer before she would be able to see her husband.

'Mr Avery took a rather nasty blow on the shoulders. He's being X-rayed, just in case of more serious injury.'

Liane's face was ashen. 'Is he all right?'

'He will be,' said the nurse reassuringly.

Grant Dubois was a small, frail figure in the hospital bed. When Liane walked into his room, her first thought was that he was sleeping. She went up to him and touched his hand gently.

'*Liefie*,' he said, and opened his eyes.

'Are you all right, Gramps?'

'Yes, thanks to Kyle. I'll be out of here tonight. It shouldn't have happened. I'm so sorry, Liane.'

She pulled up a chair beside his bed. 'I don't know anything about it. I only know there was a fire; it's as much as they told me.'

'It was my pipe,' her grandfather said sadly. 'The wretched pipe you were always scolding me about. I was in the living-room and I was smoking. I must have put down the pipe at some point, and it started smouldering, and before I knew it I was engulfed in smoke.'

'Did you fall asleep?'

'Not exactly.' He looked away, unable to meet her eyes.

'There's something you aren't telling me, Gramps,' she persisted.

'I was thinking about you and Kyle. About the friction between you. I felt responsible . . . guilty . . .'

'It had nothing to do with you,' Liane assured him firmly.

'I keep thinking that if I hadn't been so hard on Kyle maybe things would have been different. I was so absorbed in my thoughts that I forgot about the pipe. I'm so sorry, *liefie*.'

'You're all right, that's all that matters,' she said, and stroked his hand.

'Kyle saved my life, Liane,' he told her.

'How?'

'He was nearby, doing some repairs to the fence, I think, and he must have seen the smoke. I remember him running into the cottage. I could hardly breathe by that time. He lifted me in his arms and began to carry me to the door. We were almost out of the house when a piece of wood—a beam, I think—fell and hit him.'

'So that's what happened . . .'

'Have you seen him, Liane?'

'Not yet. They're still looking at his shoulders—that's where the beam must have caught him.'

'How is he?' There was urgency in the old man's voice now.

'They say he'll be all right.'

'I hope so.'

'I hope so too, Gramps,' said Liane quietly.

When her grandfather had been discharged from the hospital, Liane took him directly to High Valley. Even if the cottage had been habitable she would not have allowed him to go back there alone. She waited until he was in bed in his old room, then left him in Anna's capable hands while she returned to the hospital.

Kyle was in a bed in a ward now. His face had several long scratches, and one arm and shoulder were bandaged.

Liane sat down beside him. She tried to talk to him, to thank him for saving her grandfather's life, but his responses were brief, uninterested, monosyllabic. She told him about the cottage. It needed repairs, she said, but in time Gramps would be able to go back there again. In the meantime, she had invited him to live with them at High Valley.

'You don't mind, do you, Kyle?' she asked.

'No.'

'He's very grateful to you for saving his life.'

'Tell him not to think of it.'

'He's certain he's the cause of all our problems, and he wants to apologise.'

'It isn't important.'

'It is to Gramps. It is to me too.'

'But it isn't important to me, Liane.'

Kyle turned his eyes to the wall. Liane longed to throw her arms around him, to kiss him, to tell him how desperately she wished that the hurtful things they'd said to each other a few days ago could be taken back; to tell him that she had wanted very badly to make love with him, that she had lain awake at night in frustration.

She said none of those things. She only kissed him gently on the cheek and said, 'Goodnight; I'll see you in the morning.'

Two days later Liane drove Kyle back to High Valley. A new Kyle. A Kyle from whom all the vibrant, vital life seemed to have drained.

At night they lay together like two feelingless logs in their double bed. Kyle's injuries had healed, the doctors had pronounced him recovered, but he made no move towards Liane. He did not try to make love to her, he did not so much as kiss her. Not once did she glimpse even the slightest hint of passion in his eyes.

When a week had passed and Kyle still had shown no interest in her, Liane decided to take matters into her own hands.

One lunch-hour she found a shop that specialised in fine lingerie and bought the sexiest nightie she could find—a cheeky, provocative little garment, very short, made of a transparent black fabric and trimmed with red lace. When she put it on that night, she knew she had never looked sexier.

There was no reaction from Kyle.

Two nights later, Liane waited until Kyle was in bed and the light was out. Then she emerged from the bathroom and got between the sheets too. She waited a few minutes before moving across the bed. Kyle was lying on his side, his head turned away from her. Liane put her arm across him, quite lightly. Kyle stiffened, but lay still.

A minute or two went by, then Liane slid her hand beneath the top of Kyle's pyjamas and pressed it flat against his chest. His heart was beating faster now; she could feel the increased beat against her fingers. Still he did not speak.

She moved closer against him, curling her body around his, fitting herself against him. If he had not known it before, Kyle would know that she was naked.

'What is this?' He sounded strained.

'What does it feel like?' she whispered.

'I know how it feels, but I've been wrong before.'

'You're not wrong this time.' A slight jerkiness in her voice betrayed her nervousness. 'I'm seducing my husband.'

'Why?' His face was still turned away from her.

'I want to see my husband the way he used to be—lively, dynamic, incredibly sexy.' She drew a small breath. 'After all, he is the father of my child.'

She heard a hiss of indrawn breath as the long male body grew rigid.

'What are you saying, Liane?'

Liane felt a tensing of her own muscles, but she managed to say calmly, 'We're going to have a baby, Kyle.'

'You're *pregnant*?' He sounded awed, as if he was having difficulty taking in the news.

'That's right,' she said tremulously.

'Liane...this isn't a game, is it?'

'I wouldn't be so cruel,' she assured him.

'I don't know what to say...what to believe...'

Liane had never heard Kyle sound so vulnerable. Lifting herself on one elbow, she took his hand and drew it backwards towards her stomach. 'Feel me, Kyle. There...yes...your baby is growing inside me. Another few months and you'll feel it moving against your hand.'

'Oh, God, Liane!' Kyle, tough Kyle, had a sob in his voice.

'You're going to be a father,' she said unsteadily. 'Kyle...Kyle, won't you turn round and look at me?'

He did turn to her then. His hand went to her hip, touched it, lingered on it a moment, then dropped back on to the sheet.

'How long have you known?' he asked.

'A few weeks.'

'Why did you keep it from me until now?'

'I tried to tell you,' she said.

'You didn't.'

'Yes, Kyle, I did. I started to tell you the day I had the pregnancy confirmed, but you were so preoccupied, you had other things on your mind. You were about to go away on your business trip—remember?'

'Now that you mention it.' His breath was warm against her face. 'I think you did say there was something, but you said it could keep.'

'I thought I'd wait till you were back. I never dreamed Ingrid would be with you. And then you were always so... so busy with her. I realised the news had to wait until we were alone again.'

'And what did you do when Ingrid went?' He was angry now. 'You left me. I couldn't believe it when I saw your empty wardrobe and realised you were gone.'

'But you hauled me right back.'

'I still don't know why you did it,' he sighed.

It was so strange, lying in the dark with him, naked, talking about things they had not been able to talk about previously.

'Why did you go, Liane?' he asked.

'I'd seen you with Ingrid. You were kissing her.'

'You're crazy! We never kissed.'

'I saw you, Kyle—the day Ingrid left. I happened to be at the window that morning, and I saw the two of you in the garden. You had your arms around each other and you were kissing.'

'*That* kiss?' He sounded astonished.

'Yes.'

'So that's why you changed your mind about driving to the airport with us.' Kyle gave a ragged laugh. 'There was nothing amorous about the kiss you saw, Liane. I'd been trying for some time to persuade Ingrid to take a special managerial course. When you saw us, she'd just told me she was leaving the company so that she could begin her studies. That kiss was just a kiss of good luck between friends.'

'Are you saying I've been very foolish?' Liane whispered.

'I'm saying you misunderstood.' His hand went to her breast, cupping it. 'When you began this lovely seduction scene, you told me you had two reasons for it. One was that I was going to be the father. What was the other?'

Liane had no pride left, no reserve.

'I love you, Kyle—that was the reason. The main reason.'

His hand tightened on her breast. 'Say that again!'

'I love you, darling. I've always loved you. And I realised I couldn't let Ingrid have you—at least, not without a fight.'

He drew her against him, so tightly that she could feel the hard length of his body against hers.

'You didn't have anything to fight for, Liane.'

She closed her eyes and swallowed on a hot tide of desire. She wanted nothing more than to let him make love to her, and she suspected it was what he wanted too. But they couldn't stop talking now.

'Ingrid told me there'd been a time when you were very good friends. She hinted at a serious relationship.'

'It's true, we did have a relationship,' Kyle said quietly. 'For a time I let myself believe that we could be happy together. But then I realised that I was fooling myself. I knew that there was only one woman in the world for me, and I told Ingrid that I had to get back to her, that I'd make every effort to marry her.'

'You don't mean *me*?' Liane asked, dazed.

'Who else, my dearest love? Why do you think I was so determined to get back to High Valley?'

'But you only married me because you wanted to revenge yourself on my grandfather.'

'That was what you thought. I never said it. Not once, Liane.'

'You never denied it,' she accused.

'Because it seemed the only way I could get you.'

Liane was silent a few moments, thinking back. 'The farmers' mall. You were going to build that to annoy my grandfather.'

'Wrong. I'm a businessman, my darling. I was going to develop those fields because it seemed the practical thing to do—nothing at all to do with your grandfather. And then you came along and offered to marry me if I changed my mind about the mall. It was an offer I couldn't resist. There'd been so much strain between us. I thought if I married you, if we went on honeymoon, if I had the chance to woo you and live with you, perhaps you'd eventually learn to love me. You kept calling our marriage a charade, Liane, but it was never that for me. I wouldn't have let you go after a few years. When we spoke our vows, I meant every word.'

'I did too,' Liane said on a note of wonder.

'I love you,' said Kyle. 'I loved you when you were a young, innocent girl, and I love you even more now.'

Liane had not known that she could be quite so happy. But there was still something she did not understand.

'You've been so strange all this week, Kyle. Ever since you left the hospital you've hardly spoken to me. You didn't have any interest in touching me.'

'I'd reached the end of my tether,' he said. 'You can't imagine how upset I was when you went to live with your grandfather. You came back to me, but only because I forced you to. I finally began to believe that our marriage would never mean anything to you.'

'You were wrong there, Kyle. I was so excited when I found out I was pregnant, I felt as if we'd been given another chance. You and me and our baby.'

'We're going to be the best parents in the world,' he said against her throat.

'I love you, my darling,' Liane whispered.

'And I adore you, my dearest love. Have you any idea what it's been like this past week, lying beside you, wanting you so badly, yet convinced that you loathed me? You can't imagine how badly I wanted to make love to you.'

'How about showing me now?' she asked softly.

And for the rest of the night he did just that.

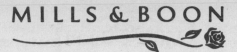

RELENTLESS AMBITIONS, SHOCKING SECRETS AND POWERFUL DESIRES

Penny Jordan's stunning new novel is not to be missed!

The dramatic story of six very different people—irrevocably linked by ambition and desire, each must face private demons in a riveting struggle for power. Together they must find the strength to emerge from the lingering shadows of the past, into the dawning promise of the future.

W❂RLDWIDE

AVAILABLE AUGUST 1993   PRICED £4.99

Accept 4 FREE Romances and 2 FREE gifts

FROM READER SERVICE

Here's an irresistible invitation from Mills & Boon. Please accept our offer of 4 FREE Romances, a CUDDLY TEDDY and a special MYSTERY GIFT!

Then, if you choose, go on to enjoy 6 captivating Romances every month for just £1.80 each, postage and packing FREE. Plus our FREE Newsletter with author news, competitions and much more.

Send the coupon below to: Mills & Boon Reader Service, FREEPOST, PO Box 236, Croydon, Surrey CR9 9EL.

NO STAMP REQUIRED

Yes! Please rush me 4 FREE Romances and 2 FREE gifts! Please also reserve me a Reader Service subscription. If I decide to subscribe I can look forward to receiving 6 brand new Romances for just £10.80 each month, post and packing FREE. If I decide not to subscribe I shall write to you within 10 days - I can keep the free books and gifts whatever I choose. I may cancel or suspend my subscription at any time. I am over 18 years of age.

Ms/Mrs/Miss/Mr _____ EP55R

Address _____

_____

Postcode _____ Signature _____

mps MAILING PREFERENCE SERVICE

Next Month's Romances

Each month you can choose from a wide variety of romance with Mills & Boon. Below are the new titles to look out for next month, why not ask either Mills & Boon Reader Service or your Newsagent to reserve you a copy of the titles you want to buy – just tick the titles you would like and either post to Reader Service or take it to any Newsagent and ask them to order your books.

Please save me the following titles:	Please tick	√
THE WEDDING	Emma Darcy	
LOVE WITHOUT REASON	Alison Fraser	
FIRE IN THE BLOOD	Charlotte Lamb	
GIVE A MAN A BAD NAME	Roberta Leigh	
TRAVELLING LIGHT	Sandra Field	
A HEALING FIRE	Patricia Wilson	
AN OLD ENCHANTMENT	Amanda Browning	
STRANGERS BY DAY	Vanessa Grant	
CONSPIRACY OF LOVE	Stephanie Howard	
FIERY ATTRACTION	Emma Richmond	
RESCUED	Rachel Elliot	
DEFIANT LOVE	Jessica Hart	
BOGUS BRIDE	Elizabeth Duke	
ONE SHINING SUMMER	Quinn Wilder	
TRUST TOO MUCH	Jayne Bauling	
A TRUE MARRIAGE	Lucy Gordon	

If you would like to order these books in addition to your regular subscription from Mills & Boon Reader Service please send £1.80 per title to: Mills & Boon Reader Service, Freepost, P.O. Box 236, Croydon, Surrey, CR9 9EL, quote your Subscriber No:.................................. (If applicable) and complete the name and address details below. Alternatively, these books are available from many local Newsagents including W.H.Smith, J.Menzies, Martins and other paperback stockists from 10 September 1993.

Name:...

Address:...

....Post Code:.........................

To Retailer: If you would like to stock M&B books please contact your regular book/magazine wholesaler for details.

You may be mailed with offers from other reputable companies as a result of this application. If you would rather not take advantage of these opportunities please tick box ☐